AT ASHVALE THE
SEXUAL TENSION NEVER SLEEPS...

ASHVALE
THE VAMPIRE'S THRALL

JADE CHURCH

THE VAMPIRE'S THRALL By Jade Church First Published in Great Britain By Jade Church in 2023

Cover design: jade church

Edited: Hannah Kaye and Noah Sky

Page Edge Design by Painted Wings Publishing Services

Ebook ISBN: 978-1-916522-03-9

Paperback ISBN: 978-1-916522-04-6

Hardback ISBN: 978-1-916522-05-3

Conditions of Sale

Content Warning

The Vampire's Thrall contains themes and content that some readers may find triggering, this includes but isn't limited to: *alcohol and drug use, murder, violence, death, blood and gore, threat, on-page sex, and swearing*

Also by Jade Church

Standalones:

Temper the Flame

This Never Happened

Three Kisses More

Sun City (Interconnected standalones):

Get Even

Fall Hard

Living in Cincy (Interconnected standalones):

In Too Deep

Tempt My Heart

Kingdom of Stars:

The Lingering Dark (Kingdom of Stars #1)

Coming Soon:

Strip Bare (Sun City)

One Last Touch

The Clarity of Light (Kingdom of Stars #2)

Keep in touch!

Don't want to miss new release details, behind the scenes sneak peeks, cover reveals, sales, and more? Then sign up to my newsletter to get swoony romance updates straight to your inbox!

https://linktr.ee/jadechurchauthor

For everyone who prefers their vampires with the humanity switch off

ASHVALE

THE VAMPIRE'S THRALL

CHAPTER ONE

LIFE SUCKS AND THEN YOU DIE. EXCEPT, sometimes you don't stay dead. It's this thought that stood out as I blinked blearily at the rows and rows of tombstones, the neat lines stretching out in front of me. I didn't know where I was. I couldn't remember how I'd got here. All I knew was that, judging by the incessant tug somewhere deep in my belly, this wasn't my final destination.

The sky was a cheery blue and the stench of pollen and freshly cut grass overwhelmed my senses, making me gag. Up until that moment, I hadn't noticed the way the sun seemed to beat down on me, making my limbs shake and my long, dark hair tremble against the ground with every strangely hollow breath that rattled my lungs.

Where the fuck was I?

The tug in my gut seemed to swell as if in answer, clenching so tightly a gasp escaped my mouth. I would have screamed if I'd had the breath. Had I eaten something bad? Was this the worst period cramp ever? My breathing sped up as I turned my head from side to side and spotted nothing

1

but more graves and grass. Biting my lip against dizziness as the world threatened to go black, I swore when something sharp split my bottom lip.

Warmth cascaded over my chin and I fumbled a shaking hand up to scrub it away, freezing at the deep red that was smeared over my palm.

My hand flew up to prod my teeth, so fast I nearly knocked them out, and I sucked in another gasp of air when I felt the odd curve of my canine as the pad of my finger split.

Had someone strapped razors to my teeth? Oh god, had I been abducted for some kind of organ harvesting? Or experimentation? But then, how had I escaped? And why couldn't I remember anything? I racked my brain, trying to remember what I'd been doing, where I'd been going, hell, who I *was* and came up with nothing.

The grave to my left was old, green growth beginning to creep over its stone base and up. If it wasn't for the oppressive heat prickling my skin and the ache in my head and jaw, it would have been surprisingly comforting, cocooned safely between the stones rising up above me. It was tempting to stay here, to just lay down and hope that my memory came back, but there was a shivery sensation that kept moving over me, like I was feverish despite my sun-reddened skin being cold. I propped myself up on my elbows and swallowed heavily when the pain that was radiating throughout my body increased. I needed to take stock of what I did know so that I wouldn't panic about what I didn't.

I was wearing plain blue skinny jeans that stretched tight over thighs that curved impressively, the waistband uncomfortably tight around the soft roundness of my stomach. A red vest top covered my top half and breasts that looked barely constrained threatened to spill over the top the longer my breaths heaved. They were clearly casual clothes, I wasn't dressed for school or for partying—in other words, there were no clues here.

The next wave of pain made me double over and I staggered forward a step without registering that I had even stood up. I careened into the tombstone to my left, rebounding to the one on my right as the pain tugged me forward and I blindly followed, shuddering when the pain eased so suddenly that I straightened in confusion. I wiped absently at my neck and then paused when I caught sight of my skin. Colourful, sweeping designs covered each of my arms down to my hands, partially obscuring my paleness. Tattoos. Roses and birds and berries and daggers, all looped together with impressive shading and pops of colour that curled effortlessly around my forearms and biceps. *But nothing that helpfully said, oh, I don't know, my name?* But then again, why would you get your own name inked onto your skin?

I lowered my arms as I scowled at the hot sun, shining cheerfully as I looked in both directions surrounding me. It was like I'd crawled out of a grave, slap bang in a cemetery in the middle of nowhere, but I couldn't see anything on the floor where I'd awakened to indicate how I'd arrived. Aside from the wind in the trees and a cricket buzzing somewhere close by, I couldn't hear or see any signs of civilisation. Was I drunk? Or on something? Was this just a seriously intense trip?

Another pulse of pain spiked through me and I hissed as I moved forwards, anything to make the unbearable ache ease. Someone was fucking with me. My hands curled into themselves, fingers digging into my palms with a strength I hadn't known I possessed as I gazed out over the headstones. I followed my gut like it was a compass, and took another step forward. The pain eased further and I took another, surer, step. Someone was fucking with me, and I was going to find out why.

A breeze kicked up and I tensed. Nothing had changed, yet I had a strong feeling that I was no longer alone.

"You must be hungry," a voice said from right beside my ear and I spun with a curse. A snicker sounded from my other side and I whirled again, the world tilting oddly like my centre of gravity had changed. That's when the scent hit me.

I saw it before I saw him.

Blood. Thick and dark. Fresh. Sliding slowly down a stark white palm and I moved forwards a step before I even registered making the decision. The stranger smirked, waving his hand like it was a treat and I was a dog, grinning wider when I followed it with my eyes. I swallowed and my tongue felt thick in my mouth, like I hadn't had a drink in months.

"Who are you? Did you do this to me?" I rasped, eyes never leaving the red spill that inched further down his forearm.

"I didn't do a thing—except watch over you until you woke up, I suppose. It was my turn to do the retrieval" I finally dragged my eyes upwards and frowned at the man standing in front of me. It hadn't escaped my notice that he'd neglected to explain who he was. Though perhaps *man* might have been a bit of a stretch. He looked maybe twenty and was made up of sharp angles. His jaw, his cheekbones— if not for the sharp blue clarity of his long-lashed eyes and blond hair, he would have been unattractive. Like a piece of artwork that was stunning in fragments and beautifully odd when knit together. The stranger cocked a smile at me and I stilled at the sight of the curling fangs that seemed to wink at me playfully. "I guess you could say I'm your guardian angel."

I couldn't hold back a laugh and it burst out of me with a startling force that made the newcomer blink and then run a hand over the short buzzed side of his head. If this man had been sent from anywhere, it was hell. His cold beauty and unnatural stillness told me that much, at least.

"You were awoken too early," he said in a bored tone, as if I was supposed to understand what that meant. "I know it can be confusing at first, but your memories will come back. If you come with me, I'll explain it all."

I frowned disbelievingly. I may have been stuck in the middle of nowhere without knowing so much as my own name, but that didn't mean I was going to follow a strange person off into the wilderness to be murdered.

"I'm good, thanks."

He snorted. "Oh yeah? And what about this?" He clenched his fist and more blood streaked down his hand, coating his fingers, and I moved forward shakily as an unbearable ache began in my jaw once more. "I think you're hungry. I think you need me. If you follow me, if you follow that annoying pull," he winked at my shocked look, "I promise everything will make sense." He waved his hand airily as the breeze shifted and the full scent of his blood hit me. I expected it to smell metallic, heavy, but instead it was light, like honey and vanilla.

A soft gasp brought me back to myself and I stumbled away, shocked, as his finger slipped out of my mouth, now free of blood. His blue eyes were still wide but something about the way he bit his lip made my senses stand to attention, like his blood had awoken something in me. A ragged breath left him and I realised my right hand was still clasped around his elbow, like I was going to restrain him... or pull him closer.

"You can trust me," he said in a low voice and everything in me ached to believe him, which was the exact reason I took another step back, letting his arm fall away from my grip. Who knew what I was feeling, or why, right now? I certainly couldn't trust some random, bloody stranger who'd approached me in the middle of nowhere and claimed to have all the answers I sought. Maybe we'd escaped from a hospital together or something—none of this made any sense.

The stranger turned his back to me, wiping his arm off on the hem of the dark distressed jumper he was wearing. "Do you want answers or not?" he called when I stayed where I was before I shuffled back several steps.

The pain in my stomach was building the further away I moved, and I cursed as it grew unbearable again, faster than before, so I began to stomp after him, the pain dulling with every inch forward.

"Good," he said, "good."

I wasn't sure yet whether or not I agreed with his assessment.

～

WE SEEMED TO COVER THE OPEN GROUND surprisingly quickly, though I had no idea how the blond stranger knew where to go. He seemed to walk without direction and appeared unbothered by the sunlight that continued to make me cranky. It wasn't pain exactly, just discomfort. Like seams rubbing on a fresh sunburn. The agony in my gut had faded to a dull ache the longer we walked, so I at least knew that the stranger was taking me in the right direction—as far as my body could tell. The absence of the pain would have been good, except it meant that my attention settled instead on the gnawing burn in my throat and my growing irritation toward the stranger.

We'd left the cemetery behind and made our way across dry grass that rose higher as we moved further in, until eventually it reached my waist and the stranger's hips.

"Do you have a name?" I asked, finally breaking the silence and he glanced back at me with a look of intrigue that instantly made me wish I could snatch the words back out of the air.

"I do."

Okay, then. "Do I have a name?"

He paused in between strides, a hesitation so slight I didn't know how I'd caught it. "You do."

"I suppose telling me would be too much to ask."

"It would," he said but I could hear the smirk in his voice and I could practically feel my blood pressure rising in response. Who was this arsehole? Why was I still traipsing after him in this fucking field? It was so noisy I could barely hear myself think, the bugs practically screamed at me and the long stalks slid across each other with a ceaseless dry rustle that was maddening. I had the urge to cup it in my palms and rip it from the ground as we moved, just to make everything shut. The fuck. Up. "Come on," he said without glancing back, and I scowled. He'd done that a lot so far, somehow knowing when I'd stopped moving or when I was hesitating without even turning around.

I grunted in response and hoped it accurately conveyed the meaning of *fuck off and die*. But I started moving again.

Whatever had happened to me... whoever had done this... it was possible he could get me answers. He certainly seemed to know more than I did right then, anyway.

I wasn't sure if I was a violent person, but considering the rage I currently harboured, smouldering hotter the longer we walked, my suspicions were veering onto the side of 'yes'.

"Where are we going?"

"Somewhere safe."

I tried to keep my tone pleasant and largely failed. "Safe from what?"

He stopped, considering my words with a gleam in his eye that made me tense as he turned to me. "From you."

What the hell was that supposed to mean? He smirked like my confusion was palpable and I closed my eyes, letting out a sharp breath through my nose.

His footsteps crunched on the dry grass as he continued walking and, after a second of staring at his retreating form, I followed.

A gleam up ahead made me squint as sunlight broke into refracted rainbows that made my head ache and eyes blur. A lake. There was barely a path around the outside but the stranger continued marching in that direction and I stumbled along after him, cursing the heavy combat boots that, though comfortably worn in, kept catching in the long grass.

"You said you were sent for me. By who? And why you?"

His heavy sigh made my teeth grind as he spun abruptly around, the amusement falling from his face as he stepped closer to me. "You ask too many questions."

"Maybe if you answered some of them I wouldn't keep

thinking of more." I scowled and was pleased that he was the one left looking annoyed this time.

"It was my turn."

His turn? I opened my mouth and he turned away, resuming his walk at an increased speed that forced me to quickly follow.

The sun felt like it was getting hotter as we walked and I groaned, my tongue feeling too big for my mouth. I was just so damn *thirsty*.

I squinted at the blond head walking in front of me. I couldn't remember why I was following him, only that I had to, but right then it didn't matter. "Hey. I don't know who you are, or what's going on here, but I need water. My throat is on fire."

He didn't stop moving and my vision blurred as I stumbled after him. "Hey! I said—"

"I heard you the first time," he said, voice casual and I frowned.

"Who are you?" I rasped and his footsteps didn't falter. "Did you do this to me?" There was a stutter in the rhythm of his feet, like he was listening to me, before he resumed his pace. "Do you have a name?" I let the tug in my stomach continue pulling me after him, my head feeling stuffy like static-filled cotton wool. "Do I?"

He shot me a look and the strangest feeling of deja vu hit me. Where were we going? Why was I following him? My throat hurt too much to ask, so I continued in his footsteps instead, hoping this wasn't a mistake.

A low *thud-thud* joined the cacophony of buzzes and chirps and I groaned, covering my ears with my hands. What the fuck was that? Some bastards dragged bongos out to the lake to swim and vibe with the earth? It was like the universe was conspiring against me, the drums beating hard behind my closed eyelids until eventually I couldn't separate it from my own pulse that seemed too quiet in comparison.

My own breathing was loud and I pressed my hands against my ears harder, the sensations washing over me in a confusing jumble that made me want to scream. But then another sound reached me. An odd gurgling, like bubbles in a can fizzing and popping and then whooshing like a great breath of air that was exhaled in one go—

I opened my eyes, finding the lake ahead instantly. There. Barely visible in the water. I didn't have time to question how I could see her, or that the drumming I'd heard seemed to be coming from her direction and was growing rapidly fainter. I just moved.

The water was cold as I dove, cooling my feverish skin that had begun to turn a light pink under the harsh sun. The water smelled like the air, fresh and clean, and like dirt. But overlaying it all was the girl whose fingertips reached desperately for the surface, finding nothing to cling to and curling limply back down.

I swam across the lake faster than I would have believed possible, but it's said that adrenaline can make the human body capable of so many things. I reached her in seconds, mere breaths, and when my head pushed beneath the surface, her eyes were already fluttering closed.

Her fingers were too thin in my hand, her pale arms too fragile in my grip. Her blonde hair floated around her, catching the light until the sunshine made it look silver. Green eyes snapped open and then rolled as I pushed us up towards the surface, snapping the reeds that had tried to entangle us as easily as swiping away a cobweb.

The air seemed cooler and the world was noisier than

ever compared to the relative quiet beneath the water, but the girl was still in my arms.

The stranger stood on the bank closest to us, watching impassively with his arms crossed as I dragged her out and shot him a glare. "Thanks so much for your help."

He said nothing, which was becoming pretty standard for him, and I scowled harder in response before thumping the girl's back once, twice, and breathing a sigh of relief when she expelled a fuck-ton of water. The drumming started up again and the sun warmed our bones and the insects screamed at me until I wanted to dive back under. To slip away and never resurface. Maybe I would have, if not for the graze on her knee. Or the scrape on her arm. Worst of all was probably the slice on her neck where one of the reeds had wrapped around her, keeping her in what would have been a watery grave. Then all I could see was red, and my jaw felt like it would shatter, and my hands turned to claws on her shoulders, her green eyes flicking open and her mouth rounding in terror as I sank my teeth deeply into her neck.

"Leonora, no!"

The words were muffled, unimportant. Heat cascaded into me like it could wash away my aggravation, my worries, and I let it, moaning deeply as the world seemed to pause before I realised the overwhelming noise had simply hushed. My throat moved as I took the warmth in and my tongue laved the skin as I pulled back, smiling at the girl who'd made the world quiet again.

But something was wrong. Her skin, already pale, was practically translucent and the blue of her veins stood out sharply. Her chest didn't rise.

I stumbled back and felt a warm hand grasp my shoulder.

The stranger. His eyes flicked once to the girl before he sighed.

"It's okay. I'll take care of it."

Take care of it? What did that mean? What was there to take care of? The stranger moved away from me and slid his arms beneath a girl, easing her up from the ground like she weighed nothing but the muscles in his forearms tensed as he cradled her and waded back into the water.

I was too shocked to speak, to ask what he was doing, until, abruptly, he let the girl go and I slipped forward a step in the slick mud we'd stirred up.

"What are you doing?" I pushed forwards, the water slapping at my calves as I splashed into the lake in loud stomps that rattled my teeth. "No, no. I-I just pulled her out. Didn't I? Didn't I pull her out? What are you doing?"

"Taking care of your mess," he snapped and his eyes seemed colder than ever as he grabbed me around the shoulders and pushed me back onto the bank.

"What did you do? *What did you do to me!*" My hands started to shake and I tugged restlessly at the ends of my hair as I watched the water ripple, a few bubbles escaping towards the surface as the girl sank once more. "I need to get her out. I've got to get her—"

"She's gone. Leave her be." His hand thunked down on my shoulder and I screamed with rage, slamming my hands backward and into his chest.

"What do you mean she's gone? I saved her! She was drowning and I saved her. I—"

"You killed her," he said, raising his arms as he got to his feet slowly. A muscle in his jaw ticked as he brushed grass off his front and pushed his hair back out of his eyes. "You ripped out her throat."

"No, no…"

"Yes. You sank in your fangs and drank her dry."

"No."

"Leonora—"

"That is not my name."

"How would you know?" he shot back and I moaned, digging my palms into my eyes.

No, he had to be wrong. I hadn't killed that girl. I'd saved her. I'd saved her.

"You killed her," he said and then shrugged. "It's okay, everyone has their first."

I screamed, rage bursting through me as I picked him up by his throat, raising him into the air and squeezing so hard his delicate face turned pink before I slammed him back down as the grass greyed beneath my feet. "What did you do to me? *What did you do?* I don't want to be a monster. *I don't want to be like you!*"

His eyes were wide as I stood over him, wrath making my limbs tremble and my anger seemed a living thing, rumbling loudly inside me, demanding I take him, sink in my fangs and—

No. No, no, no. I didn't have fangs. I didn't want to kill people. I dropped to my knees and my face tipped to the sky as the previously sunny day gave way to rain that dripped onto my face as if to cleanse me.

I'd killed the girl. I saved her, and then I killed her.

"I'm sorry," the stranger said and I blinked up at him dully, confusion swirling through me. His pale skin seemed to glow against the sudden darkness of the thunder-struck sky, lightning flashing until he seemed like some avenging god ready to cast me down for my sins. "It's better this way. Should have just done this from the beginning," he muttered and I couldn't make sense of the words. "I promise you won't feel a thing."

Reason seemed to war with my senses as he moved closer, until instinct made my muscles clench and as he snapped out his hands towards my head, I dove for his throat.

Chapter Two

I jolted awake with a gasp as a sharp crack split through the air. Cool earth pressed into my palms and I blinked slowly up at the stars. When had night fallen? Where the hell was I?

It smelled like fresh rain, lingering amidst the tree leaves that I could hear rustling somewhere out of my sight. I sat up gingerly, looking around at my new surroundings and attempting to unclench my jaw. Large gates stood off to my left, tall and black and reeking of age. From my position in the middle of some kind of woodland trail, I couldn't see very much and I could remember even less.

There was mud on my clothes and in my hair and I had no idea how it had gotten there—in fact, there were a lot of gaps in my memory. The most worrying were *who the hell am I* and *how the hell did I get here.*

A long wall spanned an entire length of forest to my right, glimpses of grey brick visible between the trees. The wind stirred faintly against the back of my neck and I whirled around to face the gate again, stumbling slightly when I moved too fast and growling when I saw who stood before me, a hazy memory knocked loose.

"You."

"Good, you woke up. I was ninety percent sure you would."

I rubbed my neck and rolled my shoulders while I scowled. "What did you do?"

The blonde-haired freak smiled before he turned away and began walking in the direction of the gates—or more accurately, the guard tower next to the gate. I raised a cool eyebrow at the enormous structure. It seemed overkill, theatrical even. "I killed you."

I stopped walking as if I'd hit an invisible barrier. "You— I'm sorry. What?"

"Don't worry, the soreness in your neck will fade soon. Probably."

I knew my eyes were likely comically wide, and I could feel the cool air on my tongue so my mouth had obviously fallen open, but all I could think was that he had to be joking. He wasn't making any sense. How could I be dead? I was standing right here, walking and talking and—

I gasped in a breath, feeling oddly hollow, like I'd forgotten to do so for a long while. I'd made a mistake following the stranger. He didn't have answers for me.

A shadowy form appeared between the stone gaps of the guard tower and I tensed, preparing to shout for help when I paused. What if the guard was working with the blond guy?

I hesitated for a second more before deciding it was worth the risk and sucking in a breath that got stuck in my throat as a hand clamped over my mouth.

"Quiet now, I'd rather not have an audience just yet," the stranger whispered, breath tickling my ear as his fingertips pinched at my cheeks. That was when I noticed the odd way the figure on the tower was slumped. *I'd rather not have an audience just yet.* Oh god. Was the guard...?

The loud crack I'd heard when I had come around flashed in my memory, the sound so clear I nearly jumped.

"Good," he murmured when I stayed frozen in place. "Now, it's my unlikely job to be discreet tonight given the circumstances of your arrival. You know, most people don't need retrieving at all—so I suppose that makes you special." Nothing he was saying made any sense to me and he rolled his eyes at the lack of comprehension on my face. "When I tell you, you're going to jump. Understand?"

Anger thawed the frozen fear stuck in my veins and I glared as best I could in the dark and he chuckled like he had no trouble seeing it.

His hand slipped away from my lips but I remained silent. If the guard was dead... Well, for now it was better to play along with whatever this crazy arsehole wanted.

He walked towards the base of the guard tower and I frowned as I followed, expecting a door to appear in the brickwork or a tunnel entrance to reveal itself. Nothing happened.

Under the torchlight that shone down to where we were standing, the stranger's hair seemed to dance with the flames and I hadn't realised how cold his skin had looked until the fire warmed it. He smirked when he turned and found me examining him but I didn't drop my eyes. Let him think what he wanted, I just knew I'd need a good description to give the police once I got away from this bastard.

"Up we go then, love."

"Up?"

The stranger winked and bent thighs that were

surprisingly built in a move that seemed too fast, but my eyes tracked anyway. I half-snorted, expecting him to go absolutely nowhere, and then choked when he soared straight up and landed on top of the guard tower wall.

"Quickly now, I'd hate to have to kill our friend here twice."

He was mad, I realised. Utterly mad. I didn't know how he'd managed that insane jump, but if he thought I could replicate it he was going to be sorely disappointed. Plus, what was this talk of killing the guard twice?

"Leonora," he demanded and I stiffened.

"That is not my name."

"I beg to differ," he sneered and my hands balled into fists. There was a smirk in his voice when he called down to me, like he'd somehow seen my reaction and wanted to push me further. "Poor little Leonora, murdered twice and doesn't even know her own name. I suppose the only upside to memory loss is that you no longer remember how pathetic I assume your life was. Of course, if you remember differently, Leonora," he said tauntingly, "feel free to correct me. At least this way—" My knuckles grazed his cheek and he grinned ferally as he tilted his face just out of the way of my strike. "Good, let's get on with it then. Down we go."

I panted heavily and then blinked when I realised where I stood, swaying when I looked down and out over the wall and at the quiet forest. Nothing moved except the pine leaves in the wind... and the ring finger of the downed guard. How the hell had I gotten up here? And now he wanted me to jump *down* the other side? I didn't have a death wish, but apparently *he* did.

"Time's up, love."

A firm hand gripped me around my waist and the other

clamped over my mouth again as the blond stranger ran and dove over the other side of the castle wall.

My shrieks were muffled and the stranger's hand clamped tighter as if in warning. Too tight, I realised, when his palm sliced open on one of my strangely sharp teeth and something hot and sweet dripped onto my tongue.

The step into mid-air seemed to last forever but also no time at all. We hit the ground with a thud and my legs instinctively bent, and the hand that had been tight around my mouth now tried to pull away but found itself caught in my vise-like grip.

"Now love, I don't think you're ready for—" his words cut off with a groan as I bit more firmly into his palm, only half-aware of what I was doing, just knowing I needed more.

"Leo–nora," he choked and the name managed to penetrate through the warm haze of pleasure briefly, something he seemed to realise. "It's too much. You're not ready."

I tightened my grip and he moaned, it was deep and rumbled pleasantly through me as I pressed closer to his arm. His head tilted back when my teeth plunged deeper, exposing the long, pale column of his throat and I paused again, distracted by something more than mere words.

Something fluttered there in his neck, like a butterfly teasing me, taunting me to try for a bite. My fangs slid smoothly out from his arm and his eyes fluttered open, glazed and heavy as they watched me. The drugged look on his face faded the longer my teeth stayed out of his body but I felt like I was vibrating, my eyes locked on that single pulse point as it beckoned me with a dull throb that blocked out all other sounds.

Clo-ser. Clo-ser. I licked my lips and let out a breathy sigh as the remaining blood was licked off. It was like the richest, smoothest chocolate I'd ever tasted. And I knew intrinsically, that if I bit right...*there*, it would taste even better.

Frantic hands grasped my jaw as the stranger tried to stop my bite and I snarled, a long, inhuman sound that startled me. Had that been... me? What the fuck was I doing?

He seemed to see the reason bleeding back into my eyes, because he let out a shaky breath that sounded a lot like relief. "Progress," he muttered. "I didn't have to snap your neck that time." I continued to blink at him in shocked silence as he carefully sat up and frowned at his hand where two perfectly even bite marks were slowly healing. "Don't do that again. It's rude to bite someone without their permission."

Rude? He thought I was rude? I mean, yes, I had just tried to go for his jugular, but he was the one who'd done this... thing to me in the first place! He'd killed the guard, he'd dragged me all the way here after the girl in the lake—

My thoughts stuttered to a stop and my hand flew up to cover my mouth as a ragged sob tried to escape. The girl in the lake. Had I killed her? The stranger was right, I really had lost myself. I had killed her. I had almost killed him. But the worst part was...*I'd liked it.*

"No time for hysterics," he said firmly, standing and looking even paler against the dark than he had earlier, like a ghost haunting the grounds of an old castle. "We've already wasted enough time."

Numb, I let him grab my arm and pull us through the grounds. He clearly knew where he was going, and I knew the smart thing to do would be to pay attention, to try and remember the direction we were walking and which door we were headed towards, but I couldn't bring myself to care.

Even if I did escape, even if I made it to the police, who's to say the one they should be locking up wasn't me?

Around the side of the castle sat a small black door, so tiny I was a good head and shoulders taller and the stranger would have to practically crouch to walk inside.

The door was silent as it opened and that alarmed me more than a horror-movie creak. It meant someone was here, someone was maintaining this door. How often did they do this to people like me?

The darkness loomed ahead and the stranger stepped back and nodded for me to go first. I stood at the boundary and hesitated, glancing back to look at the stranger one more time and finding that he now only looked tired. Losing half a pint of blood would probably do that to a person.

A torch's flame popped to my right and I jumped slightly, peering into the darkness before I lifted a foot and walked inside. The night air was calm and the stranger's eyes were bright as the door swung shut behind us, and I couldn't help the thought that nothing was going to be the same again.

CHAPTER THREE

I'D EXPECTED THE CASTLE CORRIDORS TO BE colder. Old stone bricks swept into high arches above our heads as the hallway wove onward and the stranger's steps were soft against the floor. I tried my best to minimise my own noise—which was hard in combat boots—as I took in the quiet darkness around us.

The hair on my arms stayed down and my breath never fogged, and just as I was starting to believe that maybe I would get out of this alive, we rounded our first corner. A solid wood door thunked harshly under the stranger's hand and footsteps disrupted the perfect spill of golden light as the door swung inward.

I wasn't sure what I'd been expecting, but a young, albeit slightly sickly looking, woman with dark hair and eyes wasn't it. She looked like she'd once had a full figure that had withered, her cheeks just slightly too hollow and her smile a touch too big for her face. And boy was she smiling, big and toothy, the way I imagined the wolf might have smiled at little Red when it posed as her grandmother. I did a double take at the delicately curving fangs that took the place of her canines. Any hope I might have been holding onto guttered out at that moment. This woman was with him. The stranger. Whatever they'd done to themselves, they'd somehow done it to me too.

I tensed and the blond arsehole grabbed my arm, as if sensing I had been about to bolt.

"Don't bite me again," he murmured with a snap of his teeth in my direction that made me flinch.

The woman looked on in something like amusement before stepping to one side. "Enter."

I did as she bade without too much thought, sitting myself in one of the heavy wooden chairs that was placed in front of an equally antique-looking desk before I froze. Why had I done that? Up until she'd spoken, I'd been thinking about running.

The woman laughed quietly as she moved around the desk so gracefully it almost looked like her feet didn't touch the ground. "I see we do have an odd predicament indeed. You were sent on this retrieval, Hayes?"

Finally, a name. Hayes. He shot me an irritated look, like he'd been enjoying withholding the information, before he answered. "Yes. Nobody saw us come in, as requested."

"Casualties?"

"One."

Oh god. The girl. The girl in the lake. How had I forgotten? What was happening to me? Another memory poked at the corners of my mind, another person, another bite, but it drifted away before I could grasp it.

"Hm." The woman leaned in and peered closely at my face. "What do you remember, Leonora?"

"Don't call me that."

"It is your name, is it not?"

I stayed silent and shot Hayes a glare when he smirked. "She doesn't remember."

"Anything at all?" The woman's dark brows furrowed and I found myself watching her intently. Something about her seemed... off.

"Nothing." Hayes hesitated, biting his full lower lip for a moment before admitting, "I don't think she even really remembers everything that's happened since we met."

The woman nodded. "Yes, I'd imagine the block is still in place and working overtime to erase her exposure to the supernatural, but it has begun to break down since her transformation. Poor dear," she said, turning her attention back to me, "you must be so confused."

That was when it hit me and I reared back in my seat, shocked as I spun to Hayes. "Did I... did I bite you?"

Hayes rubbed the back of his neck, looking down at the plush rug that covered the stone floor and the woman gave a low laugh.

"Oh, she's a strong one, isn't she?" she said to herself, standing up and taking my chin in her tight grip while she peered into my eyes, humming in satisfaction at whatever she saw. "You didn't feel the bite worth mentioning, Hayes? You know there are no points for this assignment, only pass or fail. She's here," the woman said, looking me up and down and wrinkling her nose slightly, "and mostly in one piece."

"I don't..." Hayes shook his head before giving me a look that was surprisingly helpless and the woman's eyes flicked back and forth between us for a moment before she laughed again, longer and harder. Somehow it chilled me more than her silence.

"Oh, this is truly delightful. I haven't seen a blood bond in years."

I flicked my eyes to Hayes, trying to see if he understood what this meant, but he was staring at the woman with something akin to horror on his face.

"We'll deal with that later," she said dismissively as she finally released my chin, only to place her fingers at my temples. "This might hurt a smidge."

A lancing heat flooded through my head and shuddered down my whole body and I would have screamed if I could have remembered how. Memories flitted past my mind's eye and I wanted to look away, wanted to forget what I'd seen as I watched the girl from the lake grow still, saw Hayes thrown into the air by an invisible hand and then crushed to the ground before the vision swapped and there he was again, on the floor panting as I took his blood from his body in large pulls that made him moan.

Things they'd said started to make sense as the part of me that had been locked away behind the mental block resurfaced. My life and memories as a living vampire, preserved until I passed the ultimate vampiric test of strength. Then the block would fade, memories finally clicking back into their rightful place as the woman stripped away the magickal partition.

I could see a dark chamber and I remembered the feel of red lace itching my much smaller body, the touch of cold stone as I was laid down and the magick that would make me forget the vampiric world until my nineteenth birthday was cast. Except, I'd never reached nineteen.

The woman's hands fell away and I heaved in breaths that burned my lungs. Hayes' heart seemed to beat too loudly in the room and I focused on it until my shaking subsided and I could look up and meet their eyes. My memories from my time as a 'human' were still a mystery, but my supernatural ones from my early life, the ones the magickal block had shielded, were very much intact.

When I'd come into this room I'd thought that I might still make it out alive. I'd been wrong. By the time I'd entered this room, I was already dead.

New knowledge burned in my brain, as well as a clearer idea of what had really happened since Hayes had found me in the cemetery. But it wasn't supposed to happen this way. I shouldn't be undead yet. Not like this. Not so soon. I should have awoken as a living vampire and made my way to the closest sanctuary, ready to complete my studies on vampirism and then chosen for myself when to make the transition from living vampire to undead. But I'd been *retrieved*, whatever that meant. All I knew was that it wasn't supposed to happen like this.

When I looked up and met the eyes of the woman across the desk, I finally realised what had seemed so odd about her —she was dead. One of the many undead vampires that likely existed in the world, a rank I had just joined. In this room, the only heart that beat was Hayes' and it would do so until his death when he would join us too.

"What happened?" I asked calmly, evenly, and the woman's smile became sharper.

"You were murdered."

Murdered. I blinked, the only sign of shock I would allow myself to show. It happened, of course, but it was rare that a living vampire awakened as an undead before their memories were returned. It was dangerous, as I supposed I had proved by killing that girl and biting Hayes, to have undead vampires running around freely, unable to control their impulses. Our race survived through secrecy. Was that why I'd been *retrieved*?

"You're sure?" The undead vampire nodded and I couldn't even look at Hayes as my world was ripped out from under my feet. "How did you know to find me?"

Her dark eyes blinked slowly at me, like a predator watching prey. "I received an order for retrieval. Rare," she explained, seeing my confusion, "but not unprecedented. As such, one of our most-promising second years was selected to recover you and bring you here."

"Who gave the order?" Hayes said and the undead vampire's gaze cooled significantly as she looked to him.

"I don't know, but it's certainly no business of yours. Congratulations on a retrieval well done—wait outside. You're to be Leonora's guide, on account of your bond."

Hayes stood, the smirk that had seemed a permanent fixture on his face morphing into a blank mask as he nodded and I felt a shadow of something like fear as the door closed and I was left alone with a vampire.

Of course, compared to the humans we probably seemed barbaric and even as a vampire myself I could appreciate that. What other race sent their children away into the world at the age of five, without their memories of their world, purely for natural selection? If you survived, then you'd earned your place in our society and would make your way to the closest sanctuary, ready for training.

"How long until my memories come back?"

"Of your human life?" The woman considered me, tapping her chin lightly with one finger. "Maybe tomorrow, maybe never. I imagine it will largely depend on you, dear."

Silence fell as we considered each other and I tried to ignore the slight dryness of my throat that had been steadily rising since the block had been removed from my mind. New vampires needed more blood than usual to counteract the effects of their death and transformation. Then throw in the effect that magick had on the vampiric body and... well, it was no wonder I was a little thirsty.

My eyes drifted to the door that Hayes had left through and a shiver of awareness coasted over my skin, like he was looking back at me from the other side.

"Welcome to Ashvale, Leonora. I trust your stay with us will be pleasant. You may call me Elowen, I am the head of the sanctuary."

My eyes pulled away from the door with effort and the sensation faded.

"In your time at Ashvale, you will make your debut to vampiric society—it is a particularly big cause for celebration when a new undead joins our ranks and this will give your sire line the chance to claim you as part of their lineage. Typically this happens once per year and you've arrived in time for our ball next month. Perfection—" Elowen grinned and I shivered at the glimpse of her fangs "—cannot be rushed. Given your predicament with Hayes, I think it best that he be your assigned guide for the first year of your stay. You will have classes each week that will train you for life as an undead, though it appears you are a fast learner. Classes are not compulsory, but we strongly advise you attend in order to make the most of your time with us." She nodded to the door and where Hayes stood beyond it. "The living vampires are strong, but even one such as Hayes can only last so long in thrall. Make sure you put him out of his misery before he shows you to your room."

I wasn't sure what thrall was or how I'd accidentally placed one on Hayes, but I would figure that all out later.

"And my murder?"

"It's being looked into," Elowen said dismissively and I nodded, unsure how much I trusted that. Vampires, as best I could remember, didn't treat death in the same way as humans—they preferred to think of it as an unfortunate necessity that could be as cumbersome as it could gratifying. It might not seem like a big deal to them, but I wanted to know who had done this to me, and why.

Taking her words as a dismissal, I stood. Awareness of my new body's speed finally sank into my brain, and I could process it in a way it couldn't before. That same odd tingle swept over my skin as I opened the door opposite to the one I'd entered and practically caught Hayes as he slumped against me.

He panted as I grasped his bicep and tugged him up, half-carrying the blonde menace away down the corridor. His skin burned with heat and I shivered as our hands brushed.

His pulse thudded unevenly by my ear and my hand tightened involuntarily around his elbow. I thought I heard Elowen's laugh as the door swung shut and we were left in a corridor not unlike the one we'd previously passed through, but better lit.

I dragged Hayes onward until his hand reached out and snagged at an alcove I hadn't noticed, halting us in the corridor before he pulled us inside.

The stone was cool at my back, but I probably wouldn't have noticed if not for the heat of Hayes at my front. He shoved away from me until his back hit the opposite wall in the tight space, chest heaving as though he fought for breath. When he opened his eyes they were clear but surprisingly bright, almost feverish.

"Leonora," he growled and I fell unnaturally still. "Please."

I didn't know what he was asking for, what he needed, but he seemed to loathe begging for it. He seemed to read the confusion on my face and his head fell back against the stone. I watched the movement of his throat in fascination as he swallowed hard, surprised I'd caught the motion in the darkness the torch-lit corridor couldn't quite reach.

The castle was silent, which I would have thought odd for vampires, except that the majority of those in Ashvale were likely living vampires who tolerated the sun much better than the undead. Hayes' ragged breathing seemed to reach a fever pitch and his hand moved so quickly that it was a blur even to me as it slapped against the stone next to my face.

"Please," he repeated, voice tight as he titled his chin and bared his throat.

My eyes fixed on the pulse thudding fast in his neck, my fingers brushing over it in anticipation and Hayes moaned breathlessly. "Why?"

His voice was a growl that was barely decipherable as he balled his hands against the stone wall. "Because we are bound, for better or worse." I didn't know what he meant, but it was clear that *worse* was the descriptor he was favouring. "I feel your hunger as if it were my own, my body aches for your bite as a result, not to mention the power you're exuding right now. So please, just fucking do it."

I swallowed as he arched his back, tilting his head further to welcome me in. The hunger rose up in me, and this time I didn't try to fight it—I embraced it.

I struck, sinking my teeth deeply into his soft skin, and flicked my tongue across his neck, repeating the motion when Hayes gasped. His hand slid from the wall and bunched in my hair, pulling me closer instead of pushing me away as his body finally relaxed.

He tasted impossibly sweet, more so than I remembered, and I let the bite turn sharp as I dug in a little deeper, the venom in the bite making him pant in pleasure until I pulled back.

I'd successfully bitten someone without killing them. Progress, as Hayes likely would have said, if he wasn't high out of his mind right then.

I waited with him until his flushed cheeks faded to their normal paleness and his eyes cleared, and then we stepped out of the alcove.

"Elowen said something about you showing me to a room?"

Hayes grunted and I followed him down the corridor and up several flights of stairs that would have winded me before my transformation but were mere blips in time now.

"Here," he said, stopping outside of a dark hardwood door and producing a key from his pocket. "You were expected." He dropped the key in my palm and turned to leave, pausing only briefly when I called out.

"Hayes? How did you find me in the cemetery?"

He tilted his head in my direction but didn't look back as he said, "We take care of our own."

CHAPTER FOUR

I'D FALLEN STRAIGHT INTO BED AFTER HAYES HAD left, the events of the day finally catching up with me. My new body was likely still completing the final parts of my transformation, it wasn't as instantaneous as the movies always made it out to be and I still felt... unsettled.

Kick-started by my death, I'd awoken. If I hadn't fed on blood, my body would have eventually withered, unable to sustain the transformation, and I would have gone mad as my brain decayed.

I laid in the cool white sheets and stared up at the ceiling as I remembered the girl from the lake. With the block on my mind firmly broken, I could now remember some of the details without the confusing jumble I'd had before.

It wasn't supposed to be like this. Whoever had done this to me hadn't only murdered me, they'd also made me into a murderer too. First feedings were supposed to be in a controlled environment, usually after the training like that which Ashvale provided. Vampires were supposed to care for those who provided for them, it was considered bad form to kill the humans you drank from. Secrecy, integrity, strength. My childhood self had received some training in the court of the vampires—their values, the hierarchy, and that in itself raised interesting questions about who my sire line fell with. Not every vampire got to experience the court, nor meet the twelve council members who each ran their own version of Ashvale in their respective territories.

Of course, it was the monarchs who had the final say and most influence among vampiric society, but as far as I could remember I'd never met them.

Even with the small amount of information I now had unlocked inside my brain, I wasn't sure what my blood bond with Hayes truly meant. I could feel him inside me, like a tiny little knot entangled next to my heart, thrumming quickly in a way that mine never would again.

I sighed, blowing out a harsh breath as I pushed out of the thick duvet and let my bare feet hit the hardwood floor. Hayes had said I'd been expected, and that I'd find what I needed inside the room, but I'd been too tired to look around much yesterday. I'd simply shucked off my boots, yanked off my jeans and climbed into bed, sans bra. But now I headed over to the armoire with more than a little trepidation, opening it to find three white T-shirts hanging up inside as well as a pair of black jeans. Basic, yes, but if they fit then I'd be happy. I didn't want to have to put on the clothes I must have died in. The clothes I'd killed in.

There was a toothbrush still in its wrapping and some cheap shampoo and shower gel in the en-suite, so I spent a long time making myself feel more human, even if I no longer was one. Even if I never had been. I ran the plastic comb they had provided through my long hair and winced as it snagged on a curl. As soon as I was allowed, I was going to have to go out and get some products for my hair or my curls would start to rule me instead of the other way around.

Things felt less unfamiliar this morning, like maybe I'd been dreaming about my human life or like sleep had somehow reacquainted me with my body.

A cheap, apricot scented lotion was also left next to the sink, sealed. The pot was laughably small and I wasn't sure if it would last to cover both my thighs and my stomach, but I knew that usually if I wanted to keep my colourful tattoos looking fresh then I needed to moisturise them.

This place was a strange blend of modern and classic. Ashvale was a literal castle, but the en-suite was fairly modern and the mirror was hot to the touch to prevent it from fogging. A pair of pale green eyes blinked back at me, ringed with black lashes still wet from the shower, and for a second I just studied myself, taking in every little detail. It was an opportunity not many people had, to see themselves unfiltered with no preconceptions of their own image. I liked what I saw.

My skin was smooth and pale in the places not covered by tattoos. The colourful artwork spanned both my arms, curling down to brush against the back of my hands, and a large piece spanned one thigh from my hip downwards, a lithe tiger's body uncurling as it struck. Possibly my favourite of the bunch was the gothic moth situated between my breasts, its wings curving beneath as its head nestled in the centre between. They were all gorgeous designs, but I had no idea what the meaning behind them was—or if there even *was* a meaning.

Vampirism didn't alter the body, only froze it in time. So theoretically I *didn't* actually need to moisturise my tattoos or do my cleansing routine, they would never fade and I would never break out. Of course, I remembered being fascinated by the magick users in our world as a child. They brewed tonics or crafted with their bare hands, mostly vanity potions that would enable some small amount of change in our frozen bodies, and there had been nothing as exciting to me. In some ways, it was infuriating that my forgotten childhood as a living vampire was now so much clearer than my recent past masquerading as a human.

I wrapped a white towel around myself and headed back out to try on the clothes Ashvale had provided, drops of water beading on the wooden bathroom floor as I walked. I wasn't sure what I was going to do after that.

One step at a time. Get dressed. Make the bed. Track down Hayes, face the rest of the vampires at Ashvale, maybe hunt down my murderer—I let out a shaky breath and bit my lip as I assessed the clothes in the mirror. *One step at a time.*

The clothes were plain, but they fit and that was the main thing. It wasn't easy to get jeans right at the best of times, let alone for a fat woman, and I made a note to find out who to thank for this blissful piece of normalcy. I had nothing else except the clothes I'd arrived in, didn't even know if I was missing things that might be important because I still couldn't remember anything about my stupid fucking life before some shithead—

Breathe.

I let out one shuddering breath and then took another. Technically I didn't need the air any more, but the rhythm was comforting nonetheless. The first few days after the change were supposed to be emotionally volatile and so far that appeared to be true, unless I was always this angry. Though, to be fair to myself, it wasn't every day that someone murdered me and robbed me of all choices in my life. I would never give birth, I would never reach twenty. My hands shook and I balled them, standing abruptly from the edge of the bed where I'd been staring absently into the free-standing mirror next to the armoire. I couldn't sit here thinking and moping and getting angry again all day. It was a quick way to get someone killed, having an angry, baby-undead vamp running amok.

I pulled on yesterday's socks, they'd neglected to provide me with any underwear —though one perk to vampirism was never having to have a period again so I supposed I wouldn't have to worry about where on earth I might be in my cycle right now. I'd never get sweaty again either. Small mercies—maybe I'd swap to an aerosol deodorant instead of the roll on I typically used, which doubled up as chub-rub. It was both confusing and irritating that I knew stupid shit like that but nothing else from my 'human' life.

I left my hair to air dry, figuring the dryer might just make it frizz more, and took another calming breath before I hauled open the heavy door and stepped out, immediately almost walking into a passing woman.

Her eyes flew wide and I could see every fleck of gold in her amber irises before I turned and locked my room with the solid iron key Hayes had given me.

"Hello," I said when she continued to stare. It was probably a shock to see such a young undead vampire, so I allowed her a few more seconds before I started to get annoyed.

I could hear her pulse fluttering and when my lips parted it only grew faster at the sight of my fangs, larger than that of a living vampire. If she was a second year student, she'd know that she was lower than me on both the food chain and pecking order. Vampires were surprisingly big on etiquette and hierarchy, and I outranked her simply because her heart still beat and mine did not.

The girl gulped and a pretty flush rose to her cheeks. Normally I might not have noticed, but the other thing that made newly turned undead vamps dangerous? We got hungry. A lot.

"Can you tell me where to find Hayes' room?" I said stiffly, trying to ignore the way my fangs had begun to ache and my hands trembled. The girl stayed quiet and I clenched my jaw before snapping out. "Now."

The command at last seemed to unfreeze her and she pointed to a staircase off to my left. It was better than nothing, so I nodded and left as quickly as I could, lest I have another... incident.

It felt like the knot in my chest that was Hayes grew warmer the further up the stairs I moved, and I was glad this bond was at least good for something. There were rows of dark wood doors just like mine, generously spaced apart in the wide corridor and I paused before one that stood slightly ajar, the knot in my chest burning as if to confirm that this was where I was supposed to be.

I nudged the door open gingerly and stopped short, my bloodlust rising even as a wholly new hunger joined the first.

I'd found Hayes, but he was... occupied. Another living vampire with dark hair grasped firmly at Hayes' pale shoulder, restraining him or holding him up, I couldn't tell, as his lips worked at Hayes' throat. It felt like my own shivered in response, remembering the sweet-as-sin taste of him as a possessiveness rose up in me, my lips lifting off of my teeth instinctively. The living vampires didn't need blood until they died and rose as an undead, either through choice or accident, but that didn't mean they couldn't indulge.

The dark-haired man moved and my eyes drifted past the lips on Hayes' throat to the cock slowly working its way in and out of his arse. Hayes flung his head back with a groan, the strong column of his throat beckoning me enticingly as a bead of blood dropped down. I remained frozen as the other man's hand traced a confident pathway down Hayes' surprisingly taught chest and down to his dick, fisting it even as the dark-haired man's hips flexed from behind.

I should say something. Or I should leave. Either way, this wasn't meant for me.

The man's pace increased, his low moans raising the hairs on my arms in a way that I found utterly fascinating. Clearly some of my bodily functions still worked.

Hayes' blonde hair was mussed and his cheeks were flushed pink, making him look oddly cherubic as his hand bent backward to grip the dark-haired man's throat while they fucked.

I took a step backwards and his eyes flashed open, the cold blue meeting mine in something like resignation. As if he'd known I was there all along and had hoped he might be wrong.

"I'm sorry for interrupting," I said as smoothly as I was able and the other man jumped, clearly not having realised I was there. "I'll come back later."

But my feet stayed rooted to the ground, like Hayes' eyes had the power to hold me there through will alone.

He slowly pulled away from the other man and didn't look back even when he murmured a protest.

"Hayes, what are you doing?"

Hayes didn't reply to the other man, just moved closer to

me. "I think I hate you," he said to me as he stood inches away, seemingly unconcerned about his own nakedness. Truthfully, he had no reason to hide. With the blood smearing his neck and the flush from his cheeks spilling down over his chest, he was perhaps the most delectable thing I'd ever seen—until he opened his mouth. "I didn't realise how different... how much *better* the bite was from an undead. The whole time his fangs were in me, all I craved was you."

A thrill swept through me at his words, even if what he really meant was that he craved my bite and not me.

I took a step closer and his eyes darkened when I lifted a hand and tilted his chin to the side, exposing the clean holes on his neck.

The other man stepped off the bed, a warning on his face that looked like it was travelling to his mouth when he got his first proper look at me and his senses told him something he didn't want to believe. He went pale, and I couldn't stop my smile.

"You're a vampire," he choked out and I licked the small trail of blood on Hayes neck, making him pant.

"Yes," I said, raising an eyebrow in question because it seemed like a given—this *was* a kind of school specifically for vampires? Then I held his eyes as I slid my fangs into the same place on Hayes' neck, claiming the mark for my own and slowly swallowing as the other man stood rooted in place. *Mine*, I thought and Hayes frowned like he'd heard but he didn't protest, just slid one arm around my waist as if the motion was automatic, tucking me closer before grimacing, like he was mad at his loss of self-control.

Whatever this bond between us was... I got the feeling it was going to be trouble.

Hayes' grimace faded, replaced by a look of bliss as I pulled from him deeply, relishing the taste of him on my tongue. I was hungrier than I thought and when I pulled back he swayed. I swept my tongue across my mouth, eager to catch every precious drop, and there was a strange smugness in knowing that I made him feel so good he would have let me keep going. Even if it killed him.

"I'm just going to leave," the other guy said and I stiffened, having forgotten he was there as the bloodlust took over.

As my emotions settled, the hunger within me sated for the time being, I could feel a little regret at my behaviour. They had clearly been... busy, before I'd charged in and taken over. But Hayes didn't protest and the air felt heavier after the other living vampire left.

"Did you need something?" Hayes said eventually, voice flat. I would have thought he was unaffected by the blood exchange except for the blush that was deep on his cheeks and across the pale skin of his chest. I stopped my eyes from moving any lower, but I would have been surprised if he wasn't hard. Bloodlust did interesting things to the body— both living and dead, it seemed.

"Well, I was mostly looking for information, but I suppose I should thank you for breakfast too?"

He rolled his eyes as he strode further away from me, like the distance would help reduce the strange pull between us. His room was similar to mine with the same mix of modernity and age. Without any self-consciousness, he stepped into some dark jeans and the sound of the zipper made me look away as I realised I'd been staring.

"I live to serve," he said dryly and I met his icy eyes before they vanished beneath the plain white tee he'd pulled on.

"I live to... Well, I guess I don't live at all," I retorted, not liking the way he watched me. Like I was somehow responsible for the bond between us. I mean, yeah, I had bitten him. But I'd like to see how his self-control was if he'd been awoken after being murdered and then someone basically dangled themselves in front of him.

"So you're saying I was asking for it?" He snorted and I swallowed the growl that tried to escape.

"No. I'm just saying—Wait. What?"

He stilled as he sat down on the bed, the rumpled covers stirring my bloodlust again as the urge to reinforce my claim on him rose up. I squinted at him but he said nothing, so I continued, unsure if I had imagined him responding.

"I'm just saying that you shoved your hand over my lips and bled in my mouth—it would have been more surprising if I *hadn't* bit you."

He snorted but didn't argue and the silence between us grew fraught, like there was a thread connecting us that had grown more rigid the longer I stayed at a distance. That concerned me more than anything. I was going to have a hard enough time keeping myself in check and stopping my instincts from ruling my behaviour, the last thing I needed was this bond making things even more muddy.

"You'll cope."

"I knew it!" I moved toward him and nearly stumbled when my new body moved with more speed than I was used to. "Stay out of my head."

Hayes scrubbed one hand over the shaved part of his head before growling out at me, "Trust me, I'd love to live my life without your thoughts accosting me, just another wonderful perk of this fucking bond."

I sighed and plopped down uninvited next to him on the

bed. It was true that he'd never asked for this, but I certainly hadn't wanted it either. "How do we fix this?"

"We don't. The bond is for life."

For life? I didn't even know him, and now we were stuck together for the rest of my undead existence? "We can't break it?"

His eyes were full of a cold anger as he stood and looked down at me. "Not unless you want to die a true death, no. Keep that in mind while you're prattling on in there," he said, pushing the centre of my forehead with one finger and I snarled.

He may have been more experienced than I was, but he was still just a living vampire. *Show him his place*, a dark voice inside of me purred and my hands curled into fists as I bared my fangs.

The muscle in his jaw feathered as Hayes tilted his chin to one side ever so slightly. Accepting my dominance, even though it clearly pissed him off.

My instincts settled down but left me feeling drained. "What does this mean for us then?" I lisped around my fangs.

Hayes strode towards his door and held it open for me in clear dismissal. "It means we're stuck together."

Chapter Five

I was pretty sure Hayes was supposed to give me a tour. But after kicking me out of his room, he'd slammed the door behind us and headed off in the other direction with a curt, "Don't follow me."

That suited me just fine, I needed some time to digest everything too, and I was more than capable of showing myself around. If anything, it was everyone else I was worried about—though thanks to Hayes and my lack of self-control I'd at least been able to tide my hunger over for now.

The hall was rich with daylight from the large window at the end of the hall, making my eyes water, so I decided to move upwards instead of heading back to my room or following Hayes. The sunlight wouldn't kill me—or, at least, it would take a *very* long time to do so. For now, it was just irritating and achy. Kind of like a bright day with a hangover. But eventually, when I was either old or powerful enough, prolonged exposure would drive my body to flame and then ash if allowed to burn. I backed away from the window with a grimace.

The corridors and staircases seemed to snake inwards in an upward spiral, but my legs never seemed to tire as I climbed higher. Everything looked the same—smooth, dark wood and old stone walls, the cool air carrying all kinds of scents to me as I inhaled out of habit. Candles burning, dust, and a darker, richer, scent that made my mouth water until I clamped it shut. Heat rose within me and I gripped the wooden handrail beneath my hands as I fought not to follow that scent and consume it. A groan cut the air, startling me and I let go of the railing with wide eyes as I saw deep cracks forming. Shit. Hopefully some gentle destruction of property wasn't a big deal.

I beat a hasty retreat just in case and nearly went dizzy with the speed of my movements before I paused at the base of the next staircase, a thought occurring to me. I hadn't chosen this for myself, but there was no undoing it now. If I was going to survive this transition, I needed to find new things to love, to live for.

I hesitated for only a second more and then let myself go, sprinting up the staircases as quickly as I could, my feet barely touching the ground like I was flying. A laugh slipped out of me as I wound higher and higher until I hit the top floor and could go no further. The room was small like an attic, but round on all sides with a high ceiling. Was I inside a fucking turret?

The window was large, an ovular frame with a ledge made of stone that was chipped on the edges, and the sunlight was irritating on my skin as I peeked out at the grounds.

I was higher up than I'd anticipated and my stomach swooped with a mixture of fear and excitement. There wasn't much that could kill me now, but that didn't mean falling from this height wouldn't hurt.

Or would it? Just how far could I push this new body of mine?

The window had an old-fashioned brass latch on one side and the soft snick of it unlatching made me glance behind at the open stairway warily. Was this a bad idea? Probably. But I was pretty sure I'd heal quickly if I had over-estimated my new abilities.

I slipped the window open and stepped up onto the ledge. Shivering with pleasure and not cold as the outside air slipped over my skin, I raised my hand to shield my eyes from the light. It stung a little more without the protection of the glass, but it was more like a light pins and needles sensation than true pain. I inhaled deeply and could taste the trees on my tongue as I looked out at the miles of forest that surrounded the castle—and took one step forward.

A hand curled around my bicep and I jumped slightly, annoyed that I'd been so lost in smell and taste that I'd neglected my other senses. Hayes was panting beside me, eyes wide as his grip tightened. I assumed he'd been able to find me the same way I'd located his room earlier—the thought didn't thrill me. Did our link fade more over distance? We were going to need to experiment.

"What the hell are you doing?"

I shrugged. "Jumping."

His hand dropped from my arm as he folded his own across his chest, his mouth flat with annoyance. "You know it won't kill you right?"

"I'm not trying to die," I said, rolling my eyes. "I was just... trying things out."

He raised a cool eyebrow but shrugged. "Fine. A little

warning might be nice though. I won't die if you do, but that doesn't mean it won't hurt like a bitch."

I narrowed my eyes. His attitude was really starting to piss me off. "Consider yourself warned," I said with as much innocence as I could muster before I moved, hauling him against my chest as I leapt off of the ledge with a laugh that turned into a scream.

This had to be what flying felt like, your hair streaming around you, eyes watering from the force of the air, adrenaline roaring through your system so hard I would probably have been sick if I was human.

The ground approached far too quickly, I hadn't been ready to leave the freefall yet. Hayes had remained silent almost the entire way down, completely expressionless until we hit the ground. I landed on my feet and the mud puffed up around me before I skidded with the remaining force from the fall. I glanced back and swore when I saw Hayes, hovering in the air lazily and a small smirk on his lips as he watched me brush mud off of my new jeans.

"How?" I demanded and his smirk grew. No wonder the bastard had seemed so calm, he could practically fly.

"Air," he said, like that explained everything. He rolled his eyes and I knew he must have heard my thoughts. "Those of us with a little more power can wield other gifts."

I crossed my arms like that wasn't super fucking cool and gave a disinterested nod. God, I hoped I had some kind of cool power. Not that I would let Hayes know he had anything remotely of interest to me.

"So what time do classes start?"

"About half-hour ago," he said with a casual shrug, that same infuriating smirk twisting his lips at my clear irritation.

"And you didn't think I'd want to go?"

"You seemed a little preoccupied by running up and down the stairs like you'd never seen a set before."

I clenched my jaw, grinding my teeth together and mentally counting to five before I replied. "You're a dick."

He shrugged and pressed a hand to his chest mockingly. "Ouch. Words can hurt you know."

I moved fluidly, my new instincts driving me more than the other way around as I closed my hand around his throat. Had I always been this prone to violence? Or was it just becoming a member of the newly undead that made me want to rip Hayes' throat out whenever he so much as made a sarcastic comment?

"Things are more intense when you un-die." His eyes were cool as he watched me like my hand wasn't slowly tightening around his neck. "Besides, you may have got the upper hand the other day, but I can take you out if I need to. Undead vamp or not."

A low laugh rumbled through my chest, and his eyes widened slightly as my lips lifted to show off my impressively long fangs. "You really think you could take me down? Might be hard to do while you're begging for my bite."

His hands connected with my shoulders as he shoved me away and I laughed, flinging my head back as I felt his irritation run through me, like a faint telephone connection filled with static between us. Good to know I could get in his head too.

"I don't beg." His nostrils flared and a muscle in his jaw feathered but I just smiled and turned away without comment, heading back in the direction of the castle.

It had definitely seemed like he'd been begging for me last night.

Hayes scowled like he'd heard my thought and I

chuckled. If he didn't like what he heard, then he should just stop listening.

His long legs ate up the distance between us easily as he outpaced me. "Come on."

"Where are we going?"

"Lunch."

"You offering?" I couldn't resist trying to rile him up. It wasn't like anything about this was easy for me either, but he was acting like I'd had a choice in our bond—or even becoming an undead.

The glower on his face didn't ease as he threw me a sour look. "Lunch for those of us who actually need real food."

"Shame," I said, snapping my teeth at him as we reached the door in record time. "I was starting to feel snacky."

I nearly stumbled when a sharp sensation rolled through me and I looked at him in surprise. Because that hadn't been irritation he'd felt at the snap of my teeth—it had been something else, something even stronger. Lust.

And he thought he wouldn't beg for me?

CHAPTER SIX

"This is probably the worst tour I've ever had," I remarked the next day as Hayes strode past open doorways and snatches of lessons reached me. I'd spent the remainder of my first day at Ashvale sleeping and testing out my new speed and strength before crashing in the evening, exhausted. "Don't you need to be in class right now?"

He threw a scowl at me over his shoulder and I rolled my eyes as he continued his strong pace down the corridor. Our footsteps reverberated slightly, like an echo travelling being consumed by the stone walls, eager to absorb any glimmer of life it could get. I tilted my head as we rounded a corner and the sound of drum-like heartbeats thudded around me. It was strange to be one of the few dead things in a place otherwise filled with life. Or if not quite life, then at the very least blood.

Just thinking the word made me swallow harshly as my jaw ached. I hadn't even realised I'd stopped in place until a shockingly warm hand wrapped around my elbow and eyes filled every inch of my vision as I sucked down rapid breaths I no longer needed.

"Leonora."

I blinked, unsure when I'd move closer to him. "Yes?"

There was a wariness in the set of his shoulders, the slant of his mouth as he dropped his hand. "You need to focus. Don't let the hunger consume you."

I nodded vaguely but my eyes had found the throbbing pulse in his neck. "Sure."

"You've made waves since you arrived as it is, what with being undead at eighteen, so the last thing you need is to draw more attention to yourself by draining me dry right now."

Draining him dry? We were *so* on the same wavelength. "Uh-huh," I muttered.

"Something's not right," he muttered but I was too lost in the smell of his warmth to pay much attention. "You shouldn't still be this hungry. What did they do to you?"

My eyes lifted to his as my hands curled into fists. "What do you mean?" This was important. I had to focus.

"The hunger in the beginning," he said, his frown taking over his whole face as spoke in hushed tones in the middle of the corridor, moments of space between us. Easily eliminated. I almost smiled, anyone looking out of their classroom would likely think we were together with the way our heads were bent towards each other. "It's been two days since you woke up, so it should be fading by now."

I pinched my palms with my nails in an effort to refocus.

"That hunger drives you to feed and repair the damage of your death. The greater injury, the more blood you need to complete the transition."

Shit. "You're saying I haven't finished the transition yet?"

He shrugged, stepping back from me. "Maybe. Either way, you need blood. A lot of it and soon, before your survival instincts kick in and we find the student body becoming significantly smaller."

I followed when he moved deeper into the castle, the corridors seeming to grow darker the longer we walked. Less windows, I realised. "And if I take everything I need from you?"

"You'll probably kill me," he said, matter-of-fact.

"So, what? Humans? Other living vampires?"

A flash of emotion down the bond came and went too quickly for me to make sense of it and I watched his face closely. Did the thought of me drinking from someone else irritate him?

"Living vampires would be better than human blood, our blood is richer. But in this case, you need something else."

What else was there?

He didn't answer the unspoken question until we arrived at a door that was vaguely familiar. No heartbeat sounded from beyond the wood. The only sound was our footsteps, catching up to us like we were being haunted by our own souls.

Hayes knocked on the door, his mouth a flat line that had me on alert. Whatever was about to happen, he didn't like it.

The door swung inward of its own accord and I raised an eyebrow when I saw a familiar desk and the undead vampire sitting behind it.

"Leonora, Hayes." Elowen smiled and the sight of her long fangs still put me on edge, recognising the bigger predator in the room. "What can I do for you?"

Hayes explained to Elowen what he'd already told me, and I watched their faces keenly while they spoke.

"I see," she murmured before rounding her desk, deep dark eyes locked on mine. She looked different than last night when I'd arrived, the hollows under her eyes and cheekbones less pronounced, her figure a little fuller and her smooth sheet of dark hair gleamed. She had fed, and fed well, it seemed. "Well, we can take care of this and then I suggest you rest for the remainder of the day. My blood will likely be a little too much for you to handle, even as relatively young as I still am."

I shot Hayes a quick look and he just watched us, his face a blank mask. "What do I need to do?"

Elowen waved a hand and a cool gust of air closed the door behind me, making me jump. I glanced between the two vampires. Hadn't Hayes said his affinity was for air too? Were they of the same bloodline? They couldn't have looked more different, but maybe he took after his father.

Elowen rolled up the thin sleeve of her black dress to reveal one pale, slender wrist. "Drink."

The command in her voice would have made me move even if the call of her blood hadn't. Thankfully my body seemed to know what to do and my fangs lengthened, puncturing her skin neatly.

The first drag of her blood I nearly choked. It was thick, and rich, like Hayes had said. It felt like acrid fireworks on my tongue, burning and blazing as it moved through my veins and I dragged harder.

"That's enough." Hayes' voice barely registered and I bit harder. "You only need a few mouthfuls, Leonora. If you take too much you'll become unstable, your body won't be able to handle the power."

I could hear him, I could even logically see that he was right—already I could feel Elowen's power moving through me, heightening everything until I could count the dust motes in the air. But I couldn't let go. My jaw wouldn't obey, my throat still swallowed greedily. I couldn't stop.

My eyes opened and found Hayes' watching us. I didn't want to beg him for his help, but I couldn't bring myself to pull away and Elowen had gone limp as the enzymes from my bite washed through her.

Two fingers on my jaw pressed hard until I pulled free and spun to confront the one who had interrupted us. I panted as I licked blood for my lips and Hayes watched me warily as Elowen swayed in place before sitting down heavily against the top of her desk.

I felt strangely unhinged, like I'd been blown wide open as more energy than I could ever remember having felt lit me up.

"Rest," Elowen demanded, but her voice was weak as she tried to stand tall. "Classes can wait. I'd rather you not be in a classroom with what's coming next."

I'd slowly relaxed the longer she'd been talking, a heat curling around me that made my skin feel like it was buzzing.

Wait, what had she said about something coming next?

"Get her out of here," Elowen said and Hayes nodded, the movement jerky as he gripped my arm and dragged me out of the room. I gasped as his fingers on my skin felt like the height of pleasure and pain, like my nerve endings were alight with sensitivity.

"What's happening to me?" I gritted out between my teeth and he didn't reply, just tightened his grip and suddenly we were moving faster, practically flying through the corridors until we were back at my bedroom door. It slammed behind us before I could even register that we'd moved inside. The key turned in the lock and I tensed, my legs widening as I attempted to brace.

"Trust me," Hayes said and when I didn't relax he rolled his eyes. "The lock is for your own good."

"Maybe I want to decide that for myself."

"You won't be in any mind to decide anything for a while."

I hesitated and then let my stance ease before retreating to sit on the edge of my bed. He watched me warily, expecting... something.

"Explain," I demanded and he sighed, kicking off his boots before coming closer.

"Drinking the blood of an undead can have... side effects."

"Bastard," I muttered. "You didn't think to tell me this before?"

He shrugged. "It wouldn't have made a difference." His eyes were steady as he assessed me but they felt strangely like a caress on my skin, like he could see to whatever lay beneath the surface of my flesh to the no-longer-beating heart of me. "You needed the blood, we'll just have to deal with the consequences."

"There's something you're not telling me," I murmured as I kicked off my own shoes and crawled to the centre of the bed, raising up onto my knees so I could peer into his eyes. His breath feathered across my mouth and I shivered. "Why do *you* need to be here? Why is the door locked?"

"You're going to need me."

I drew back sharply. "I don't need you for anything."

"Are you sure about that?" This time it was him who leaned closer, his fingertips brushing over my knee and sending hunger thudding through me. "You forget, we're connected, Leonora. I can feel what you feel, to an extent, and you're about to be feeling... a lot. I'm duty-bound by the bond to be here."

"What does that even mean?" I snapped, not liking the way he was acting like he had no choices here. "Just get out. If you don't want to be here, then go."

"I *need* to be here," he said, voice harsh and the sound of it, rough and hoarse, was driving me insane.

I growled at him, my fangs still elongated from drinking from Elowen. "Get. Out." I moved closer and let him see the threat in my eyes. I could feel the predator lurking beneath my skin and I wasn't sure I could hold it back even if I wanted to.

He laughed and the sound was a low rumble that made my nostrils flare as he moved back into my space. "Make. Me."

My hands fisted in his t-shirt and I felt a spring in my muscles, like I had strength that was just waiting, begging to be used. But instead of throwing him out, my body had different ideas.

I dragged him against me and snarled. "Leave."

"No," he murmured simply and this time I yelled in frustration before driving my lips against his. God, what was I doing? What was happening? The tether between us that I recognised as our bond was taut, lit up like it had been doused in gasoline and we'd just lit a match.

Hayes' mouth was savage, hungry, punishing and I kissed him back just as hard.

"I don't like you," he panted, voice hard even as his lips moved back towards mine. "I don't trust you." A hard kiss took our breath away as his teeth clashed with mine and my lip was caught between his as he tugged. "But I'm stuck with you, and right now the heightened blood lust you're experiencing is drowning me."

I shook with need that I couldn't distinguish, was this lust or hunger? Or were they one and the same?

"We can pretend we're in control," he continued, his voice so low and guttural that it would have sent me running if I had been human. "But this blood between us owns our souls—*you* own my soul—and right now there's nothing I can do about that except keep you in here with me."

"Because the bond protects you somehow?"

He nodded, his mouth too busy travelling a wet path over my throat as his hand fisted in my dark curls to reply.

"But it wouldn't protect them," I said, nodding to the door he'd locked and he nodded again, his hands spanning my waist like he needed to touch all of me. The feeling was, unfortunately, mutual. What a locked door would really do to keep me in here was negligible, but then I suppose that was why Hayes was here, distracting me.

"How long until it fades?"

He shook his head and I arched beneath his touch. Fuck. This didn't have to mean anything. People fucked all the time and it didn't mean anything. But we weren't going to go that far, were we?

"What would happen if you drank from me?" My voice was breathless and he froze above me, sitting atop my thighs as he looked at me, eyes darker than usual.

"Right now, it might kill me."

"Or?"

"Or we'd make the halls bleed red." I considered that with a tilt to my head and he smiled slightly. "I'm not going to drink from you, and not just because you're chock full of Elowen's blood."

"Why then?" The burning in my veins was fading and he'd noticed it too.

"It's like I told you before," he said as he tugged my hands out from under his shirt, and swung his leg over me to climb off of the bed. "I don't like you."

Fucker.

"I think the worst of it has likely passed." He moved away from the bed like it was on fire and I grimaced, attempting to sit up and shocking myself when I couldn't. My body felt heavy, like I was being pinned down by the air itself.

My eyes narrowed. "Are you doing this?"

He shook his head as he tugged his boots back on. "You need to rest. Your body is crashing. Sleep, Leonora."

I wasn't sure why I obeyed, but my eyes slid closed and the last thing I heard was the click of the lock in the door as Hayes left.

CHAPTER SEVEN

By the time I woke, it was dark. I wasn't really sure how I could tell the sun had gone down—maybe it was a vampire thing. Like an itch under my skin that I hadn't realised was there until it was gone.

From what little I could remember from my childhood, I knew it would only get worse the older I became. The sunlight affected all undead vampires to an extent, but age and power played the biggest part in how well it could be tolerated. I hoped it was a long way off for me though, I would miss the sun eventually. I'd been a little uncomfortable outside earlier, after I'd jumped from the tower, but I didn't really have a gauge to compare the discomfort to know whether it was normal for an undead as new as me.

I stayed in bed, staring up at the ceiling for the better part of ten minutes before restlessness made me swing my legs out of the covers. There was too much zipping around in my brain and I needed to clear my head—a walk sounded like the perfect way to do that.

The corridors should be largely deserted; classes were held during the day as the vast majority of those attending were living vampires who had no problem with the sun. I could only assume some of the instructors had to also be living vampires too, though perhaps not. Undead vampires weren't always the most considerate or empathetic type, so making the classes during the day regardless of discomfort for an undead instructor wasn't too outside the realm of possibility.

Either way, I was hoping that I would be able to wander around undisturbed as I tried to force my mind to stop overworking itself. But really, there was a lot to process. I was a *vampire*. Not only that, I was *dead*. Someone had murdered me, and clearly in a pretty horrific way if what Hayes had said was true. Without my memories, it was hard for me to know what I might have been missing out on, what dreams I still carried unfulfilled. There were things I was starting to love about being a vampire, but reconciling who I was becoming with who I used to be felt like I was betraying human-Leonora. Like if I enjoyed myself for even a second, I was lessening the weight of the choice that had been taken from her—me.

I closed my bedroom door behind myself as quietly as possible and then made my way down the corridor, the cold air not bothering me even in my sleep shorts and tee.

Then there was my death itself. I was circling over the same thoughts over and over, wondering if I'd deserved it, if it had been a justified death—or even how they'd done it. Was the trauma of my death really the culprit for my missing memories? I rounded the corner and my pace picked up until my bare feet began to thud quietly against the stone floor.

Would my bloodline still claim me even if I'd technically

failed the ultimate vampiric test of strength? I hadn't been able to survive on my own—but I was pretty sure I hadn't been far from my nineteenth birthday when I'd died. Would they think that was close enough? Would they consider me one of them, or a failure? And did I care if the latter was true?

My hair stirred in the breeze I was creating as the walls passed me in a blur of speed as I ran up and down the stairs, through the winding corridors and then came to a fluid stop beside one of the windows overlooking the greenery and forest below.

I looked out at the swaying trees, breathing in the unique taste of night-time. How had I managed to get so close to Ashvale? Had I already been on my way here while I was alive?

The forest didn't have any answers for me, and I sighed as I rested my chest lightly against the slate window ledge. If I squinted, I could almost pretend that I could see the lake from here—the one I'd killed the girl in, covering myself in blood and muck from the water—

I tilted my head as something occurred to me. I had been murdered, apparently in a way so brutal my body had needed more than the usual amount of blood to finish my transition. So why hadn't I woken up covered in my *own* blood? Somebody had to have cleaned me up. Maybe they'd even dumped me closer to Ashvale, which meant that maybe my murder hadn't been as random as I'd initially assumed.

Or maybe I was just tired and spiralling. I wasn't a detective, I knew nothing about murders, let alone how to solve one. But if I was a pawn in someone else's game, well, that I would need to deal with.

I turned from the window, deciding I could probably try

to sleep some more, when something stirred in the trees.

My head whipped back around and I froze as whatever it was stopped and turned, like it could sense me watching.

I chanced a slow lean forward and managed to catch a glimpse of silvery fur highlighted by the moonlight before the animal disappeared. I blinked and leaned slightly out of the window to look around, but couldn't spot whatever it had been. I'd never seen anything like it before and whatever it was, it had moved so fast I had missed it. That creature was as fast as a vampire. Maybe faster.

A knot of worry began to form in my stomach as I turned away from the window and slowly made my way back to my room on the third floor. Why did I get the feeling that things were only going to get worse before they got better?

Unbidden, my mind found itself on Hayes. It was understandable, he was clearly an example of worse rather than better and what we'd done earlier... Well, it wouldn't be happening again. We'd only done what we'd had to do to protect everyone else and appease the monster in me, driven wild by Elowen's blood. Unfortunately, we were stuck together and I had the irritating suspicion that I was going to need him if I wanted any hope of surviving this place, especially if there was a chance that something supernatural had played a hand in my death. Who was to say they wouldn't come back to finish the job?

With that cheery thought in mind, I ran all the way back to my room in just a few seconds without even breaking a sweat. I locked the door carefully and ignored the pull of the bond that wanted me to find Hayes. I'd seen more than enough of him for one lifetime—the bond didn't agree but, as I climbed into bed, I decided that was a problem for tomorrow.

Chapter Eight

I ACTUALLY MANAGED TO GET TO CLASSES THE NEXT day, no thanks to Hayes. He'd walked past me as I'd left my room and looked straight ahead, not saying a word.

Thanks to my late-night wandering the night before, I was pretty sure that Hayes didn't need to pass my room to get to his classes. So he'd deliberately gone out of his way to ignore me—I just wasn't sure why. Did he think I would be trailing after him like a love-sick puppy just because of some kisses?

The vampire leading our introductory session—Lark—was living and looked to be around mid-thirties, so unless he was planning on dying twice and never living as an undead he would probably transition in the next ten years or so, while he was still young enough to be healthy and further his sire line but not so young that he'd be ID'd buying booze for eternity. I'd noticed him shooting me wary glances since I'd arrived at the door just off of the second floor corridor staircase.

The other students weren't much better. Some radiated

fear and mistrust, but others had undisguised interest that was off-putting instead of enticing. It wasn't often that living vampires became undead so young. When it did happen, things tended to get messy—as Lark was demonstrating for them now.

He gestured to the wall behind him where a projector broadcast in wobbly lines onto the stones. "Without the proper preparations and training, and given the typical trauma of the living vampires affected by an early death, it is usually safest to terminate the newly undead rather than attempt to corral them. Though, of course, there are exceptions."

I raised an eyebrow. This only reaffirmed what I'd been wondering since last night. Undead baby vamps, especially those disoriented by the magical block like I had been, didn't usually make it to these academies of training. But I had. Someone had wanted me here, but to survive? Or to direct me like a loose canon at whoever they had wanted dead?

I pinched the inside of my cheek as I tried to recall something, *anything*, from my death. Several pairs of eyes had turned my way at Lark's words but nobody voiced the very thoughts running through my head—why was I still here?

Lecture on that particular subject apparently done with, Lark cleared his throat as he clicked a button to change the projected picture from one of bloody carnage to some kind of basic powerpoint with three images: the sun, the heart, and the head.

"There's not much that can truly kill an undead vampire —even their living counterparts are remarkably resilient."

I was beginning to think of this class as Vampires For

Dummies, because who didn't know the ways to kill a vampire?

"What about fire?" A slender looking living vampire in the row ahead of me called and Lark's nose wrinkled. The micro-expression was so quick that I was sure none of the living vampires had caught it. Lark thought this kid was an idiot too, and that made me feel better for some reason.

"Harder to regenerate and recover from, especially if the vampire is already in a weakened state. But with enough blood, there isn't much we can't heal as long as the fire doesn't fully destroy the heart or head."

Interesting. I was now virtually indestructible then, as long as my head stayed on my shoulders and my heart free from pointy objects.

I tuned Lark out as he began to move on to vampire hierarchy and politics, paying just enough attention to level a hard gaze at some of the living vamps who tried to stare me down when Lark mentioned the position the undead held over the living. One girl in particular seemed a little more hostile than the rest for whatever reason and I flashed her a little bit of fang in warning, satisfied when she dropped her head and turned around stiffly.

There were only newly awoken living vamps in this class, plus me. Those a year ahead had different classes than the basics I would have to go through, so I would have to wait to talk to Hayes about my suspicions. I didn't necessarily trust him, but I needed more information than I had right now and with the bond between us it was in his best interests to keep me alive. I was pretty sure anyway.

The lesson wrapped up and the group of us began to shuffle towards the door. Newly awoken living vampires turned up at Ashvale most days and I couldn't imagine anything more miserable than giving that same introductory lesson over and over for eternity. I wondered if it was some kind of punishment decided by the council of vampires who held court. The good thing about Ashvale was that this wasn't a school, technically—there weren't any grades or passing or failings, there was just information, training. If I wanted to survive in this new world then I needed to arm myself with as much knowledge as I could. But while sanctuary attendance was mandatory, Lark had explained, I was under no obligation to actually participate. So with that in mind, I skipped our next class in favour of finding Hayes. I wasn't sure that it could wait any longer, not if I was right and someone or something had done this to me deliberately, had let me survive when I should have been put down, and they were either here with us, or had deliberately sent me here in the hopes of... something.

A familiar figure appeared ahead of me, and I followed as Hayes walked in the other direction. I rolled my eyes. He knew I was here. With the bond humming happily between us there was no way he didn't.

I appeared by his side, using my speed to catch up to him. "I need to talk to you."

"So talk." His eyes never once strayed to my face, he just stared straight ahead as we walked on.

I grabbed his arm and pulled us to a stop, tugging him into the alcove nearby. "This is nostalgic."

Hayes scowled, turning to walk away when I grabbed him again.

"Oh get over it. We kissed a bit. It meant nothing. You're still an insufferable prick and I'm not suddenly falling to your feet. I need your help."

A spluttering noise came from our right and I blinked in

surprise at the girl from Lark's class. Clearly this was the reason why she'd seemed to dislike me more than the others —I had something she wanted.

Hayes raised an eyebrow and I dismissed the girl without another look as I spoke quietly. "I don't think my death was some random thing. I think something or someone from our world was involved."

"And why would you think that?" The doubt in his voice only fueled my fire and I examined my nails as if bored while I spoke to him.

"I shouldn't be alive. Rogue undead are put down, but I awoke clean and unmarred within spitting distance of Ashvale, and you heard Elowen—someone gave the order for retrieval rather than death. You even said that you'd been expecting me!"

"Because it was close to your nineteenth birthday, not because we knew you would be murdered." He rolled his eyes and I bit back my frustration.

"Look. Are you going to help me or not?"

"Not."

I gaped as he stepped out and away from me, continuing to walk on, unhurried.

"The bond means this affects you too! Especially if someone wants to come back and finish the job," I called after him and he stilled.

"It's not enough. There are a million possible reasons for everything you just said. You need more evidence because without it you have nothing."

"You don't think I know that?" I hissed as I found myself in his space. "I don't know where to start."

His eyes assessed my face, his mouth tightening and then relaxing as he seemed to realise I wasn't going to drop this.

"Motive. Who would want you dead? Or maybe the better question, who would want you alive?"

"You think my bloodline—"

"It's possible," he interrupted and then shrugged . "You'll find out at your debut I suppose, if they decide to claim you for their line."

"And if they don't?"

There was a flicker of pain in my chest that didn't belong to me and I frowned as Hayes began to walk away again. "There are worse things in life."

Once awoken, all vampires living and dead had their debut to be presented to the monarchs and council. It was a chance for the vampiric parents to claim their wayward children, if they found them worthy—in this world, your bloodline meant a lot when it came to your reputation and respect owed. For some, being claimed by their sire line was about power, for others it was a homecoming. A reunion. I wasn't sure what the future held for me and my heritage, nor what I hoped might come of it.

Hayes' response told me at least one thing about him that I hadn't known before: whoever his sire line belonged to, they hadn't claimed him. With our bond binding us for as long as we lived, he would be counting on my sire line claiming me if he hoped to have any power or respect within the vampiric world. Without it, they just might eat him alive.

Chapter Nine

I wasn't really sure how I was going to get any evidence to support my theory about my death—maybe Hayes had been right, maybe I was looking for something that wasn't there and should just be grateful that I had this second chance.

I grimaced as I pushed through a heavy wooden door and then stopped in awe. I'd figured there had to be a library here somewhere, so I'd wandered around and just followed my nose until the scent of old paper, dust and wood had reached me.

There were towering stacks that stretched up high enough that I had a momentary worry about being crushed should they fall. But then I remembered I was already dead and unless a stray bookshelf went through my heart or took off my head, I would be just fine.

Though, that wasn't to say it wouldn't still hurt like a bitch to have a bookcase full of philosophy texts fall on you.

I wasn't looking for anything in particular, though a family tree or genealogy book might have been handy. I couldn't force my blood-relatives to accept me, but I could make their life difficult if they shunned me. I smirked slightly as I pulled out a promisingly thick book.

Sometimes you had to take your wins where you could.

I wound my way through the stacks until I came to a small clearing, cosy and shielded on each side by more shelves. The lamp was on, a warm glow spilling out over the hardwood tables and the living vampire sitting there, hunched over the book.

"You'll hurt your neck sitting like that," I said before I could stop myself. Vampires and jokes about necks... Some people were testy. I could only hope this guy wasn't one of them. He looked up and I froze. "It's you."

Warmth coloured his cheeks but faded rapidly as he smiled slightly. It was crooked and I found myself staring at the odd tilt to his lips, entranced.

"I'm surprised you recognise me with my clothes on," he quipped and then cleared his throat. "Sorry, that was supposed to be a joke."

I smiled and nodded to the seat opposite him, a good few metres of distance away—enough that he wouldn't feel too concerned about my presence, especially considering the last time he'd seen me I had been claiming his bite mark on Hayes' neck for my own. "Can I join you?"

"Sure." He cleared some of the books scattered across the centre of his workspace and nodded towards the seat I'd indicated. "I'm Rowan, by the way."

"Leonora."

Silence settled between us but I didn't feel any pressure to break it, just watched him as he watched me. Assessing. Interested.

"So you and Hayes," he began and I shrugged.

"The bond was an accident."

"Not typically."

I raised an eyebrow and he bit his lower lip before relaxing his shoulders. "Do you know why blood bonds are rare?" I shook my head and he continued, "It's because they're the closest thing we have to soulmates. There's a spark, an essence in you both, that is cut from the same cloth —like two pieces of a whole."

"I don't think I believe in soulmates." Or, at least, if they did exist I was certain that Hayes wouldn't be mine. He knew how to kiss, I'd give him that, but that didn't make him any less intolerable.

Rowan shrugged. "It's not a matter of belief. It just is."

"You're saying that you know definitely, beyond a shadow of a doubt, that blood bonds came about because of a soul-deep predisposition?" I snorted. "Even saying that aloud sounds ridiculous. Besides, Hayes is an arsehole."

Rowan laughed. "He's a little prickly on the outside."

Prickly seemed mild. It was more like an entire cactus. Lodged somewhere uncomfortable, judging by the scowl that seemed to constantly be on his face.

"Sorry, I probably shouldn't be bad-mouthing him in front of you, huh?" I mused and he shrugged.

"It's not really like that between us." At my disbelieving look he smirked. "I know how that sounds given what you walked in on. But it's true. There's nothing going on between us, not any more."

"Fair enough." The quiet fell over us again and only the soft creaks of the wind and shelves settling disturbed the sound of Rowan's heartbeats. "Are you scared of me?" I asked, genuinely curious and he laughed. The sudden sound took me aback and I stared with wide eyes until he stopped.

"A little. You could kill me in the time it takes me to blink."

"True," I allowed. "But I won't. Cross my heart," I said, unable to stop the rueful twist of my lips, "hope to die."

He laughed and the sound made my smile grow bigger, it was like a glimpse of normalcy—an unintentionally cruel taunt. Would I ever laugh like that again? Carefree?

"So what brings you to the library anyway?" I raised an eyebrow and he snorted. "I mean, aside from the books in general."

"Boredom. Research. Mostly I'm just nosey."

"You sound just like a kitten." The smirk on his face heated his dark eyes and when warmth swept through me, I was surprised. I guess having the bond didn't mean I would only be attracted to Hayes. Given the choice, I wouldn't touch Hayes with a ten-foot pole, though that was mostly on account of his attitude and not his looks.

I decided not to answer his subtle flirtation, unsure how I felt about it or him. "I figured I'd look into genealogy, what with my upcoming debut."

Rowan nodded. "Someone you're hoping for?"

"Not really, I can't remember everyone. I guess it wouldn't be bad to be a royal."

Something flashed across his face and I sat up, intrigue sparking. "What was that?"

"What was what?"

"I mentioned the royals and you became... I don't know. Amused? Concerned?"

He shrugged lightly and placed a bus ticket stub into his book. "I don't know what you mean."

Fine. I'd let him keep his secrets—for now. "Not a fan of the monarchy?" I teased and he looked at me in surprise.

"Wow, you weren't kidding about your memory."

I frowned as I stood, pushing back the tiny chair that would have cut off my butt's circulation, had it still existed. "No shit. What am I missing?"

Tucking the book under his arm, he swept the others into a neat pile—clearly I'd stumbled on his reading spot. "It's just that they don't really exist any more."

"What?" I was genuinely shocked. How could so much have changed in the thirteen or so years that I'd been gone. "What happened?"

"Nobody knows. One day they were here, the next they were gone."

"Dead?"

He lifted one shoulder and dropped it as he stepped away from the table without looking at me. "Presumed."

"You don't agree?"

He seemed to hesitate but then stopped before the entrance to one of the stacks. "I think it would take a lot of work to just vanish one of the most powerful bloodlines in our history."

"Or someone even stronger," I murmured and he nodded.

"Or that," he agreed. "Either way, the dead have a nasty habit of coming back around here."

"I'll try not to be offended that you called me nasty."

He laughed. "Well, there's always one exception to every rule." He didn't wait for my reply before his tall form disappeared into the stacks and I heard his heartbeat fade away as he left the library.

I turned to the book I'd left on the table, and climbed on top of the wood to read it. I wasn't going to subject my body to that tiny chair again. Curiosity driving me, I used the index to flip to the page mapping the monarchy and traced the lines with the tip of my fingers. It was one of the oldest and strongest lines of vampires in existence—some even thought it was the start of the vampire origin—which was why they worked in conjunction with the council to 'rule'.

There was a line beneath the most recent of the monarchs, indicating a birth, and I frowned as I took in the date. Whoever this child had been, they would have already turned nineteen. Were they dead or vanished with the rest of the royal family? Or were they out there somewhere?

It felt like there were just too many threads, too many strange and seemingly unconnected mysteries occuring at Ashvale and the larger vampiric world as well, and I'd only been there a few days. My head was spinning as I scanned the names over and over, none standing out to me. But maybe it wasn't all so unconnected—my recollection of the council chamber, my death and the lengths someone went to to ensure that I didn't *stay* dead...

If the dates were slightly inaccurate in the recording, which was a big if, was it possible that I could be the missing child? It would definitely explain the interest someone or something had taken in my welfare, but I was still lacking the thing that Hayes seemed to believe mattered most: motive.

CHAPTER TEN

MORE CLOTHES HAD BEEN LEFT IN MY ROOM yesterday evening when I'd arrived back, like some weird fairy godmother had sensed I was going to run out of plain tops soon. How they'd got into my *locked room* was a question for another day. Either way, I was more than grateful to wear something a little different, selecting a bright red vest top that made my tattoo sleeves pop.

I didn't have a class until the afternoon so I'd lounged around in bed all day, looking through the genealogy book and trying to find any spark of familiarity among the names. So far, nothing had come to me.

Given how he'd reacted yesterday when I'd been heading to class, I was shocked when I opened my door to find Hayes waiting outside.

"Creepy much," I muttered and his face remained blank. "What do you want?"

"I'm coming to class with you," he said, voice even and deep, and completely at odds with the emotion I could sense coming from our bond. I couldn't pinpoint the actual emotion, it was like a wave I could easily drown in, making me dizzy.

Hayes' hand on my arm centred me as he peered down with something almost like concern before he let go like my arm was on fire. "Let's go."

I didn't say anything, just followed him down the corridor to the stairs that would take us to the classroom I'd been in yesterday. But, to my surprise, he led us outside instead.

"Where are we going?"

"Out."

I rolled my eyes. Dick.

A small smirk ghosted across his mouth like he'd heard my comment and enjoyed it, and I didn't want to look into that too closely. I had enough on my mind.

"Why are we going *out* when the classroom is back there?"

"They'll be out here too in a minute. The fresh air helps people stay in control."

I swallowed hard. Great. I could admit that the thought of losing myself like I had when Hayes had found me was terrifying. I had murdered an innocent girl. I'd attacked Hayes. He was an arsehole, but he didn't deserve to have his throat ripped out—mostly, anyway.

The main doors to the castle were open and we stepped out onto the green without seeing anyone else. Maybe everyone knew to steer clear of this area for newbie feeding day.

The cool air hit me and I relaxed slightly before immediately tensing again when Hayes turned to face me, taking in my bare arms and the designs that intertwined on them with something unreadable on his face.

"Don't embarrass us."

"Me?" I scoffed. "Right. Sure. I guess killing you would only be a minor issue. Slight embarrassment."

He rolled his eyes and didn't have time to reply before the rest of our class filed out. Lark wasn't there this time and I felt my brows furrow in concern. They weren't going to let us try this without supervision, right? Living vampires didn't *need* blood, but they could still fall into bloodlust and drinking blood could be pleasurable for each party too. It would be far too easy to lose yourself.

Hayes stepped closer, like he could sense my worry, and I looked at him in surprise. He stared straight ahead, studious and seemingly oblivious. A moment later Elowen strolled out of the castle doors too, clad in dark jeans and boots similar to mine. She smiled around at us as she took her place before the class, but there was something cold, stilted about it. Like she'd forgotten how to feel long ago and had just been going through the motions ever since. I could only hope that I wouldn't become like that—empty, distant. That wasn't living, not really.

"You're very philosophical in the morning," Hayes muttered and I hissed at him, making his body shake with concealed laughter at my side. Bastard. How was it fair that he could hear my thoughts whenever he wanted and yet I could barely work out what he was feeling? "I'm older," he murmured before Elowen started speaking. "I have more power, more skill, and a natural affinity for telepathy."

Showoff.

"Good morning," Elowen said, clasping a black umbrella above her head to shield herself from the weak sunlight attempting to filter through the thick grey clouds. "You'll notice these sessions are outside. We've found it to be a successful method of helping contain any group bloodlust. That said, please do your best to stay in control and remove yourself from the immediate area if you become overwhelmed." Nods responded to her words and she smiled slightly, revealing a glimpse of fang. "Very good. For this exercise you will begin in pairs of your choice. Leonora, you will work with Hayes from here on out due to your bond."

Great. I hadn't expected any less when I'd found him outside my door, but it worried me nonetheless. Things between us tended to get a little... tense, when blood was involved.

A small shuffle broke out as the group found partners and we lined up as directed, facing each other.

"Excellent. Now, in your next session we will teach you how to enthral your chosen." Chosen. Such a diplomatic way of saying *victim*. "But for now, we want you to focus on your control and this will be easier to do if your partner isn't quite as agreeable."

Enthrallment—was that what Elowen had mentioned in her office my first day? Everything from that day felt like a haze, an uncomfortable blur, but I was certain she'd mentioned me accidentally enthralling Hayes.

"Unless you're aiming to kill, the first thing you must do is be aware of your chosen. Their heartbeat, their breathing, this will be easier when your senses become heightened as an undead. Close your eyes, familiarise yourself with your chosen until you can pick their heart out from a crowd."

Didn't all hearts sound the same? I closed my eyes nonetheless and focused on Hayes in front of me, the bond giving me a better-than-usual sense of him. Now I was focusing on it, I could even parse out some of what he'd been feeling before. Excitement. Anticipation. A small slither of fear, but not of me. Rather, *for* me. He was worried about what I'd do if I lost control and killed him. That it would... hurt me.

My eyes flew open and Hayes' were already on me, the ice in them having thawed slightly while he'd watched me.

"Step closer to your chosen once you're sure you're in sync with them—their breaths are your breaths. Their heart is your heart."

My heart no longer beat, but I could feel Hayes' inside me, like it could work hard enough for the two of us.

"Take in their scent. If you go too far and you lose control, their scent is the first thing that will change. Fear is tangy, you will learn to recognise it."

I shivered at the smile I could hear in Elowen's voice and forced myself to refocus on Hayes. It was probably easier for us than the others in the class. He already felt as familiar to me as my own mind. *Soulmates* Rowan had said. I still didn't believe in them, but maybe he'd been onto something.

"Let your focus shrink down. It's important to stay aware of your surroundings when feeding as this can be a vulnerable moment for us, but for today you can entrust your safety to me."

I let the bright grey-blue of Hayes' eyes swallow me whole as his heart sped up. There it was again. Anticipation.

The scent that was uniquely his—honey, dark chocolate, all things that made my mouth water, undercut by something clear like mint, was dragged in deep. My gums ached at the prospect of tasting him again.

My hands had found his chest and I stood on my toes just slightly to better reach above the place where his neck and shoulder joined.

"And when you're ready..." Elowen's voice drifted to me as if in a dream. "Bite."

I bit. Striking so quickly I was unsurprised when Hayes jolted, but I could tell from the way his heart slowed that the pinch of pain was quickly overwhelmed by the pleasure as I pulled from him. He tasted better than I remembered, like he was changing and evolving just like me, or maybe my senses were just better since I'd properly finished my transition.

His blood hit my tongue and I gasped, clasping him closer, needing more. His hand wrapped itself around my waist, tugging me roughly against his chest like a twisted embrace as I dug my teeth in harder. If my ear hadn't been so close to his mouth, I might not have heard his groan. His heart was steady, his scent the same—this wasn't fear then. He wanted this just as much as I did.

I pulled back slightly, the thought sobering me, only to find his arms like a cage around me, clasping me desperately to him. After a moment, he seemed to come back to himself, like he'd realised that now he was the one who'd slipped. I got the feeling Hayes didn't like to show weakness, and emotions were akin to the same thing. Not that it made a difference to me, I could feel him regardless of how quickly he shuttered his expression.

"Good," Elowen said and I jumped, not having realised she was behind us. "How do you feel?"

"Okay." I shrugged. I felt like I had a burst of energy, but it was nothing like the high after drinking her blood. I opened my mouth to ask how she had recovered but a snarl cut me off before I could voice the question.

Some of the group were still feeding, others were done

and were lounging on the grass looking relaxed, even a little giggly in some cases.

The snarl had come from the girl who'd glared at me the previous day. Her partner's throat was ragged, blood soaking his front and his dark skin strangely pale. She'd lost control. Luckily the majority of the group seemed too high to react to the blood. It smelled good to me, but the thought of someone's sloppy seconds didn't appeal.

Elowen grabbed the girl by her arm seemingly effortlessly, her hand pale against the charcoal grey of her jumper. "Novalie. Enough."

It was like Elowen may well have not existed as Novalie thrashed to get back to her partner who had since sunk to his knees. Elowen let the girl go and instead approached the guy who was clumsily trying to stop the blood from pouring out of him. Elowen removed the hand gently and pressed her own wrist to his mouth.

My own watered in response, remembering the electricity that had flown through me as a result of her blood.

The bleeding slowed and then stopped and as Elowen sat back and stood, the skin knitted over, smooth and healed beneath the wet blood on his neck. Amazing.

Novalie stumbled forwards, whatever Elowen had done to stop her from moving now worn off, but she didn't approach her partner. No—she came for mine.

Her fangs seemed almost comical compared to my longer set but I couldn't laugh right then, not as instinctual rage flowed through me that she would dare try to take what was mine. This wasn't careful or controlled, this was pure instinct, a force bigger than me driving me forward before I even decided to move. She'd leapt into the air, throwing herself at Hayes, but she never made it. My hand closed around her throat in the air and as she choked, her eyes cleared, the bloodlust abating at the sight of the bigger predator with its fangs at her throat.

I could kill her, I realised. The bones in her body were so fragile, it would take barely any effort at all. But was this what I wanted? To kill because I could? *Not just because you can*, a little voice inside me pointed out, *because she tried to hurt him*.

"Leonora." Hayes' voice was cool, collected, and it allowed reason to overrule the monster raging inside at the perceived slight.

I uncurled my fingers one at a time and Novalie gasped for air as I tried to convince my body to move away, to step back, and that her neck looked fine at its current angle anyway.

A small lip twitch let me know that Hayes had heard that particular thought but I was so tired I couldn't bring myself to feel anything—not shame, not amusement. Just a gap that echoed inside me that felt a lot like the place where my heart used to beat.

CHAPTER ELEVEN

YOU'D THINK IT MIGHT HAVE BEEN AWKWARD TO have lunch with the person you'd almost killed earlier that day. And maybe it was a little, but that was the good thing about vampires—violence was often deemed par for the course, especially when in the grip of bloodlust. So maybe I'd lost control of myself, but so had Novalie, and, after a tense nod, we sat at the long table together as Rowan filed in next to us, Hayes reluctantly joining a moment later.

I didn't need to eat anymore and didn't really feel any desire looking at the thick-cut sandwiches the living vampires had on their plates. I'd already had my fill, thanks to Hayes during practice. He did look a little pale, now that I thought about it.

"Can I get you anything?" I said and his eyes narrowed.

"Why?"

Rowan snorted. "Charming as ever, Hayes."

The exasperated look they exchanged intrigued me— there was definitely a past between them, but Rowan was right, there was no tension. No longing looks. The most I could pick up on through the bond was a fondness Hayes felt for the other vampire.

"I'm sure Leonora was just being nice," Rowan continued and Hayes snorted at the same time that I did.

"See." He pointed to me with a twist of amusement in his eyebrow lift. "Even Leonora knows she's not nice."

I rolled my eyes, tending to agree, except I sort of *had* been trying to be nice.

"Maybe she's just not nice to you," Rowan said, a warmth in his eyes that surprised me.

Hayes leaned across the table to peer at him closely. "Oh? And you know her so well, do you?"

Novalie looked as baffled by this turn of conversation as I felt. Her eyes looked wide in her slim face normally, but now they were the size of saucers as she darted her gaze between the two men.

"I just thought you looked a little peaky," I cut in and immediately regretted it when both of their eyes turned to me, the intensity would have made me sweat if such a thing was still possible. "I figured grabbing you some orange juice or something was the least I could do after drinking you dizzy earlier."

Hayes dropped his gaze, picking up his sandwich and chewing lazily as he looked back up to watch me, one eyebrow slightly raised.

Bastard. This was what I got for being nice—scorn.

The most visceral reaction came from across the table though, Novalie glaring at me until I turned to face her fully. I'd resisted the urge to snap her neck once today already, I wasn't sure I'd have the same patience if she tried something else.

"What's your deal," I remarked and she flashed pink and then pale.

"I don't know what you mean."

"If looks could kill I'd be dead twice," I said, reaching onto her plate and munching through a crisp. It tasted like cardboard. I reached for another one and hid my smile when she caught my wrist between her pale fingers. "You want him."

Her eyes slid to Hayes, who was watching with a blank disinterest, before nodding once.

"Have him," I forced myself to say, shrugging nonchalantly even as the bond twisted in my chest, the urge to take back the words and punish her for the thought of taking him was nearly overwhelming, and I remained silent as I battled internally. "If you want him, then take him," I challenged, raising an eyebrow tauntingly.

Novalie's eyes, a warm brown, flashed with understanding. Sure, she could try to take him if she wanted. But I would crush her. I wouldn't have a choice—there was only so much I could do when it came to pushing down the urges of my new nature. And if she fought me... she wouldn't win.

"Understood," she said, and the tension faded. I smiled at her, a hint of fang on show, and she smiled back as Rowan and Hayes watched in bemusement.

"Women are strange creatures," Hayes muttered and Rowan nodded in agreement.

"What's so strange?" I took an apple slice from Hayes' plate, relishing the irritation that flared across his face. "She wants you, or at least her vampire side likes that you're strong. I don't want you, but I don't have much choice in the matter. We're cool, it's not personal." I gave them a shrewd look. "Women do have more important things to think about than men, you know."

"You do realise I'm not some collectible to be traded at your amusement," he pointed out and I shrugged.

"If the shoe fits."

"Well, now we're all friends," Novalie said and I smirked, "maybe we should all go together to pick out our outfits for the debut."

"We're allowed to leave?" I wasn't sure why that surprised me, but I'd just assumed we would have to stay here for the full two years. LIke well-kept prisoners.

"Of course, but first years have to be accompanied by a professor or second year. Helps keep casualties to a minimum."

I nodded absently and let Novalie carry the conversation as I ran my eyes around the rest of the room. There looked to be about a hundred or so of us in the room, not including the instructors, and I was sure that more students were off elsewhere rather than eating in the large hall.

Just like before, there were a few long looks of either intrigue or distrust aimed my way, but I didn't concern myself with any of that. It was interesting how quickly some of them had formed groups not dissimilar to ours.

"Do you guys remember your past?" I said and Novalie looked surprised, clearly having been in the middle of saying something. "Sorry," I said with a grimace. "Lost in my own thoughts."

"Our past as a human?" Novalie said, clearly willing to cut her own thought off to see where mine would lead.

I shrugged. "In general."

"Yes," Hayes said and didn't elaborate further.

Rowan nodded slightly. "I don't remember much from

before," he said and I knew he meant from before he was dropped into the human world. "But I remember my life as a human. I was a student." He smiled ruefully. "Philosophy and comparative literature."

I thought back to his stack of books in the library. *Yeah, that tracked.* He seemed to read my thoughts on my face and ducked his head to hide his smile.

"I remember my parents," Noavlie said quietly, and captured all my attention. "Montreau line. I hope they come out to claim me."

I couldn't reassure her really, I had no way of knowing what other vampires would or wouldn't do, but I reached over and gently squeezed her hand anyway.

She looked surprised but then smiled shyly, tucking part of her blunt brown hair behind her ear. "What about you?"

I tried to keep my frustration hidden. "Snippets from before, the rest is a blank."

"Maybe you could try a spell?"

I blinked. "A spell?"

Rowan frowned. "Magick is dangerous for anyone untrained. You shouldn't mess about with that stuff."

"But it might help her remember something," Novalie argued and I was impressed with how vehemently she defended me. When this girl went all in, she clearly didn't mess around, I thought as I watched her admiringly.

Rowan opened his mouth to reply but Hayes cut him off. "It could be worth trying. But you should go to a professional." His tone brokered no argument and I nodded thoughtfully.

"And how would I find a professional?"

"I know a guy," he said vaguely and I wanted to laugh. Of course he did.

Rowan still looked concerned but stood before I could say any more about it. "Just be careful. There might be a reason your mind isn't ready to remember."

Well, my mind would just have to deal with it. I needed to know what had happened, who I *was*. Most importantly, I needed to know if whoever had killed me would be trying for a second, true, death.

Concern lit up the bond and I jerked my head to Hayes but found him watching Rowan's retreating form. Good, I wasn't the only one who had found his abrupt departure odd.

"So," Novalie said, clearing her throat. "Shopping?"

"I'm down," I said and elbowed Hayes hard when he didn't reply, until he begrudgingly nodded. "When do you want to go?"

"We've got plenty of time so I don't think we need to rush," she said thoughtfully, biting her bottom lip in thought before nodding decisively. "But we could leave sooner to grab you some essentials? And speak to your expert," she added with a glance at Hayes.

"Sounds like a plan." In truth, I just felt relieved to be doing *something*—every day it felt like the truth and the person I used to be slipped further away.

"This weekend?"

"Um." I wasn't actually sure what day it was now—dying tended to mess with your sense of time it seemed.

"It's Tuesday," Hayes said and I would have been annoyed that he'd read my thoughts again if I wasn't so grateful to have the info.

I nodded. "The weekend works for me."

Novalie grinned and the glint of her fangs made it wicked. "Then it's a date."

Chapter Twelve

I'd seen Hayes in our feeding sessions but he'd been strangely absent from any other part of the castle, almost like he was avoiding me. Which was laughable because he was in my fucking head all the time, lurking in the shadowy corners of it and listening to my thoughts.

If either of us had really wanted to, we could have hunted each other down easily. He was like a prickly awareness under my skin that couldn't be scratched or washed off.

Unsettling.

So I didn't seek him out. Instead, I saw him in my class, drank from him until he clutched me to his body like he never wanted to let go, and then I pretended like he didn't exist.

I'd seen Rowan in the library a few times but only in passing, like he'd heard me approaching and had decided to run. That was probably the most odd thing of all—Rowan had been nothing but friendly. Even a little, dare I say, interested? Now it was like I had the plague. The only person who didn't seem to have a sudden aversion to me was Novalie, and that was hilarious considering the rocky start to our relationship.

"Now almost everyone has themselves under control during bloodletting, we can work on some of the other key skills a vampire needs to survive."

This sounded promising, and I perked up from my position next to Hayes as Elowen looked around at us. She was right, other than one other incident we'd all managed to bite, feed, and stay in control. Which was good, because if one more living vamp had ended up nearly drained I was pretty sure Elowen would have ripped out their hearts herself. She seemed the type.

Hayes coughed and I glanced at him in surprise, seeing the grin he was smothering. Clearly he'd heard my thoughts and agreed.

"The next thing you will need to know is enthrallment— better known as thrall."

I paid attention, interested to know where she was going with this. I had no real idea how to do a thrall, despite having accidentally used it on Hayes previously. Like most things with being a vampire, I had to imagine a lot of it was about instinct.

"A thrall is good for many things: remaining undetected amongst the humans, gaining or retaining secrecy as you move throughout the world, and, of course, exercising your will on others." A few looks of concern appeared in the crowd of us and Elowen smiled slightly, the chilly one that raised the hackles on my back. "Of course, enthrallment can be a huge violation of trust, free will, and if done incorrectly can be catastrophic. We advise that this is a tool you use with discretion and delicacy."

She'd added the warning almost as an afterthought, which didn't comfort me very much. But Elowen was right, it was a useful skill to learn, even if it was morally questionable.

I raised my hand and her piercing eyes fell on me. "Yes, Leonora?"

"Is it possible to resist a thrall?"

Something lit up her eyes, like this was a question that intrigued her—and that intrigued me in turn. "In time, and with enough power, there are those that are able to resist enthrallment, but be advised that this is rare. Typically, it is harder to enthral a fellow member of the undead than a living vampire or human."

I nodded thoughtfully and she clapped her hands together, signalling for us to form our neat lines facing one another as usual.

"You will each take a turn attempting to enthral your partner. Enthrallment itself isn't difficult, it only takes focus and desire. But giving clear instructions, free from loopholes where necessary, is the hardest part."

Hayes looked more than a little wary as I approached him and looked into his eyes. I was getting good at this part of the feed—whether that was because I was more attuned to Hayes than a normal person would be, I wasn't sure. But it was easy for the world to fall away, for the trees to fall silent, for the bottom to drop out from my feet so that only his breaths, his heart kept me anchored.

"Clear commands," Elowen called and I frowned as I tried to decide what to get Hayes to do before smirking as a thought occurred to me.

I took his chin in my hands, sensing he was going to look away and make this ten-times harder for me to stay connected. "Look at me," I murmured and let my hand drop away when his head stayed where it was. "Good. Drop to your knees for me now."

I'd deliberately not muted his emotions, wanting to see the anger on his face as he obeyed. He didn't disappoint. Slowly, like he was fighting my will against his own, he folded his legs so that his knees hit the grass and his body was before mine. A muscle popped in his jaw as he glared up at me. There was anger there, definitely, but there was something else too, something that surprised me. His eyes flashed in warning and I let my smirk grow but remained silent. "Now, I want you to apologise for snapping my neck before. Be sincere. Really feel it."

The change was instant. His eyes softened, his mouth relaxing out of its usual scowl as he reached for my hands and took them in his. The warmth surprised me, he was like the sun, burning hot while I lived in shadow.

"I'm sorry for what I did to you," he said simply, lowering his eyes for a moment and when he raised them again my lips parted at the dampness on his lashes. "It was the only thing I could think to do in that moment to stop you from running away in bloodlust and doing something you might regret."

I stared at him. "Enough." My voice was hoarse and I cleared it as I looked away. This was supposed to be fun. Petty revenge. It wasn't supposed to make me feel *things*.

I heard him stand and I dropped his hands like they burned before stepping back. I had done it, enthralled him, and it felt as disgusting as I'd imagined it would.

"My turn," he said, voice gruffer than usual and I took a breath I didn't need before looking up at him.

His face was blank, wiped free of whatever emotions he

was feeling—and he was feeling a lot, I just couldn't work out what they were.

"Leonora," he said, stepping close enough that I could smell the soap he'd used that morning. "Jump as high as you can."

It was a strange feeling, the thrall. Like a suggestion tickling at the corner of my mind, almost like it was one of my own thoughts. Except I could tell it wasn't. My legs crouched before I could remember telling them to do so, and then I paused, straightening without completing the move.

Hayes tilted his head. "I told you to jump. Now."

The strange thought that was mine-but-not was back again, more demanding this time and that... pissed me off. I mentally flicked it aside and stayed standing still.

"Interesting," ELowen murmured as she watched us. "I think your technique was fine, Hayes. I think the issue is with Leonora." The undead vampire stepped in front of me, cutting off my vision of Hayes as her face swallowed the space in my eyeline. "Jump." Power filled the word, like it was coiling my muscles for me, readying me to move, and then they relaxed again as I swiped at the command mentally.

The corner of Elowen's mouth lifted as she watched me with something like pride. "A rare gift indeed, " she murmured. "I wonder if perhaps you were able to be commanded previously because your transition was still incomplete."

I shrugged. I didn't really care about the why, if this meant other people couldn't get into my head and control me then I would take whatever I could get.

"Did you notice any difference in the thrall on your end, Hayes? Did your bond affect it in any way?"

Through the gap over her shoulder as she turned, I saw

Hayes. His lips were pressed tightly together, as if deciding whether or not to tell the truth. "Yes," he admitted finally. "I could feel the thrall suggestion separately in my thoughts. I think I could have fought it if I wanted to."

And yet he hadn't. Why? I stared at him, confusion and surprise clouding my thoughts.

"Try again," Elowen commanded and Hayes wavered before attempting to walk to me. "Enough. Interesting. I could feel your struggle to resist. It seems that perhaps you can borrow some of Leonora's talent through the bond."

"How is this possible?" I finally managed to ask and Elowen smiled, showing nearly all of her teeth.

"You must have a strong bloodline indeed," she murmured and I frowned. "I do suspect that you may be one to watch, Leonora."

Somehow that didn't make me feel better.

Elowen clapped her hands again and all heads turned to us. "You've done well. Enthrallment is taxing on our energy and our personal magic source. You need to replenish this as soon as possible. Living vampires, that means food and rest. Leonora—"

"Got it," I muttered and tried to ignore the desperate ache in my fangs and the way my body seemed to hum at the thought of sinking into Hayes once more. Fuck, I really hoped he hadn't heard that particular thought.

Dismissed, the class began to walk away, probably heading to the hall where a food spread would be laid out for lunch. I didn't move, and neither did Hayes. Even when we stood alone on the grass, I couldn't bring myself to look at him.

"Come on." He held out one hand and I looked at it for a

second before taking it and allowing him to take me further from the castle and into the shade of the trees.

"You need blood."

"You need food," I pointed out and he shrugged.

"I'll eat after."

I waited another second and then hesitantly stepped closer to him, backing up until his back was against the bark of the tree closest to us. The scent of earth, rain and Hayes filled my head and I swallowed hard as he tilted his head to one side, inviting me in. The push and pull between us was driving me crazy—especially because I knew it was all down to the bond.

Making me want him. Making this feel like... more.

"What are you waiting for?" he rasped. "You want me to bleed myself for you too?"

I scowled. At least whatever I was feeling faded quickly whenever he opened his fucking mouth.

I gripped his shoulder and he winced slightly until I loosened my fingers. "Sorry," I murmured, my voice falling into a lower register I didn't entirely recognise as all my attention centred on him.

Rain began to hit the ground around us, the soft drops sounding like a thunderstorm with my sensitive hearing but I tuned it out, too caught up in the way Hayes' breaths had quickened.

"You can lie to yourself," I murmured, my lips a breath away from the skin of his neck, "but you can't lie to me. Not when I can feel how much you want this—need this." I laughed and it was low and cruel as I let my hunger take over. "Need *me*."

His mouth opened to protest as his head whipped toward me. He didn't get far.

I growled, catching his chin in my hand and thrusting his face away until he was back in the submissive position from before.

"This is mine to take," I breathed and he didn't protest. "Tell me. Say it."

"It's yours." He sounded resigned but I could feel his anticipation, his arousal, mounting through the bond. I smirked. No, he couldn't hide that from me. He liked it when we were like this. For that matter, I was pretty sure I did too.

I struck, my fangs sinking deep, and we both groaned at the same moment. Maybe it was what he'd told me, or what I could feel from him, but this feeding felt different. Deeper. Wilder. In class he'd stood still, holding himself in place and firmly in control until eventually the crest of pleasure broke him and he caved.

This time... he didn't even try to stay in control. His hand reached up and fisted my dark curls, clutching me to him, urging me to drink deeper, to take more. I obeyed and as my tongue flicked across his skin, his thigh slid between mine. The trouble with the bond was not just that I could feel his emotions, pick up on a few stray thoughts, but his lust fed mine, the wild looseness he felt was trickling through to me too. And when my hands tightened on his shoulders the bolt of pain and pleasure that slid through him lit me on fire. I pulled away, licking his blood from my lips and for a beat our eyes met and held.

His hair was mussed and damp from the rain as a sheet of it fell between us and the rest of the world. The occasional drops hit us, sliding off the edge of the branches above our heads, and I was surprised they didn't turn to steam from the heat Hayes was generating.

When he stepped closer, I was expecting it. I didn't move away, didn't flinch, and when sparks erupted through the bond, we both shivered. His hands were my hands and mine were his. There was no conscious decision that could be attributed to only one of us, there was no me or him—there was just *us*.

Our lips met and it was feverish, his teeth on my mouth, tugging at my lips roughly until I was certain that if I'd had a heart it would have been beating out of my chest.

Warm hands traced my curves, following the softness of my hips and around to squeeze my ass and the want that slid through me was frightening, or it would have been if I hadn't been so entangled with Hayes. All I could do was hold on, kiss him back just as hard, encourage his tongue to move against mine as the scent of the forest and Hayes overwhelmed me.

"This is mine to take," he said suddenly and I panted, desperate to reclaim his lips but he turned my chin with one finger. "Say it," he taunted and I swallowed, trying to think clearly around the bond and what it wanted me to do.

"It's yours." The words had barely left me when Hayes teeth were at my neck, his smaller fangs still able to pierce my skin easily and I clutched his shoulders as his thigh slid between mine once more. He dragged and my nerve endings came alive. I could see how someone could get addicted to this, the high, the *pleasure*.

His mouth worked at my throat and I moved against his thigh, needing friction, needing something. Anything.

He bit deeper and a small flare of pain shot through my shoulder, stiffening all of my muscles with remembered fear.

My hands hit his chest and the snarl that rumbled out of me sounded more like something from a lion than a girl. I widened my stance, ready for him to attack, but he just stood there, blood smeared on his mouth, watching me.

"Leonora, he said softly and something stirred in me at the name. His blonde hair stuck up at odd angles, the strands marred with blood, leaves, and dirt. "Talk to me," he said and when he took a step closer, I let him. My thoughts cleared abruptly, the fog of fear falling away as quickly as it had come. I swayed and nearly fell, but solid arms came around me and held me up until I looked up into eyes that had become unbearably familiar.

"What happened?" His voice was low, soft, but I could hear the dangerous undercurrent. For better or worse, he was my chosen and I was his. He wasn't going to let anyone hurt me, and the bond was likely giving him an insight into what I was feeling right then.

"When you bit me... At first it was good. Really good." There was a smug pleasure in the curve of his mouth at my words so I hurried on with a slight glare of warning. "But then it started to hurt and I remembered..."

I bit my lip and his nostrils flared, the urge to protect surging through him so strongly that even I could feel it.

"What did you remember, Leonora?"

"I think I remembered my death, the fear I felt," I whispered and he pulled back slightly, surprised. "I think a vampire killed me."

Chapter Thirteen

"So what, suddenly you believe me?"

Hayes shot me a look I could only interpret as *shut up, I havenoflaws*. "I never said I didn't believe you before, I was just pointing out that it was a lot of conjecture and not a lot of evidence." I stared at him in silence for a second before letting my weight sag back into his bed.

"I feel like that's the longest sentence you've ever spoken to me."

He rolled his eyes and I had the strangest urge to smile. We were very carefully not talking about what had happened outside. That was then, this was now, and truthfully I didn't think either of us knew what to do with it—with each other —or our bond.

"What you felt when I bit you," he said, and there was a careful coolness in his tone that tip-toed around the elephant in the room, "you couldn't fake that. You were lost in your base self—-something triggered your fight or flight," he added, seeing the small frown I couldn't hide as he explained.

"So it was a vampire who murdered me," I said slowly, a

little disbelievingly despite the fact that it had been my theory originally. It just sounded... different, more ridiculous, when spoken aloud.

"Probably." Hayes picked up his phone from the bedside table and gazed intently at the screen as his finger moved soundlessly. "At the very least, something about what happened outside triggered your subconscious."

"Is that... common? Like, do vampires have rules about killing other vampires? Would my vampire have known what I was?"

Hayes shrugged. "An undead vampire might have recognised what you were, but a living vampire... probably not. Murder is frowned upon, but we don't have laws in the same way the humans do—violence is often seen as a tool for solving problems."

Understandable. I watched him scroll, growing increasingly irritated the longer he was absorbed in the screen as I started to fully understand the merits of murder. "What?" he muttered, clearly feeling it through the bond.

"Well I just found out that whoever killed me might be coming back for round two and the council wouldn't give a crap about it and you're, what—playing Candy Crush?"

He closed his eyes and clenched his jaw and I could practically hear him attempting to count to ten in his mind. "Are you always so—" he struggled for words for a second before settling on, "annoying?"

"I'm annoying?" I snorted and swung my legs over the side of the bed. "It must be nice to lack so much self-awareness."

"Funny, I was just thinking the same thing about you."

I found myself at his door with barely a second passing,

but it didn't disorient me as badly this time. My body was becoming my own again.

"Prick," I hissed and flipped him off as I threw open his door and felt a thrill of satisfaction when it hit the wall behind the hinges. I didn't bother to close it, just stalked off in search of somewhere quiet where I'd be less inclined to murder people.

It was strange, really. I didn't want to kill indiscriminately and what had happened to the girl in the lake when I'd first awoken... I shuddered. I'd tried to save her and had instead killed her. I still felt remorse about that, of course, but the longer I spent as an undead, the more I felt myself settling into this new skin. Death was a part of life, natural if sometimes cruel. It alarmed me a little that killing and violence didn't seem as wrong to me now as it had when I'd first arrived at Ashvale a little over a week ago. I may be dead, but I was still changing. I just wasn't sure if it was for the better.

The door to the library crashed open harder than I'd intended. I hadn't even realised I'd been sprinting through the halls, my feet barely touching the ground. I wasn't winded, there was no burn in my lungs or sweat on my face —and there never would be again. I supposed that in a lot of ways I was grieving for a life I knew I'd had, even if I couldn't remember it.

Maybe that made it worse, in some ways. I couldn't look back on the good memories or feel relief for leaving behind the bad. It was all blank, other than the terror I'd felt when Hayes had bit me. I didn't want that emotion to be the only thing I had of my life before I'd become... this.

I stopped abruptly, blinking when Rowan jumped at the sight of me. Clearly I'd been moving so quickly his hearing hadn't picked me out. Or maybe it was the headphones he was pulling out of his ears, because it didn't seem possible that he hadn't heard the library doors slam.

"Hey, you okay?"

I bit my lip and swore when I nearly bit right through and a trickle of blood dropped onto my chin.

Rowan stood, alarm flashing across his face as he hurried around the edge of the table to stand close to me.

I closed my eyes, loving the heat from his body and the smell of ocean and sweetness he seemed to exude. I couldn't feel the cold, and yet I somehow craved the warmth, like something inside me instinctively knew I would never again be truly warm.

"What happened?" he said softly and the tension in me drained away as his hands rubbed soothingly across my upper arms.

"It's just... a lot. All of it."

His fingers moved down until they slid through mine. "For what it's worth, you're adjusting well. Not everyone has to go through what you are, but it's still jarring for most of us to find out we're not who we thought we were."

"The person I'm becoming... scares me," I admitted and when I looked up, his eyes snared mine until they dropped to my mouth—no, my chin and the blood still smearing it.

I reached to wipe it away and then stopped, curiosity burning through me. How much of what I'd felt with Hayes was about the bond versus the blood?

I tipped my head up in offering and Rowan's eyes darkened.

"What are you doing?"

"I have no idea," I murmured and he licked his lips, the

scrunch of his eyebrows making it look like he was in pain as he held himself still.

"Are you sure?" he said hoarsely and I nodded.

"Yes."

"What about Hayes?"

"What about him?" Anger raced through my veins like fire. I may have been forced into this bond with him, but Hayes didn't own my body, mind, or blood. I could choose what I did and who I did it with.

A full body shudder worked through Rowan and, for a second, he swayed closer before pulling away.

"I feel like this would be a mistake," he said and my stomach dropped with what I wanted to be disappointment but what felt a lot like relief.

"You're a good person," I said, trying not to wrinkle my nose. That was where he and Hayes differed, I supposed. Hayes would have bled me near-dry and smirked as I sat on the edge of death.... and I would have loved every second of it. Maybe we were a match made in heaven—or, more likely, hell.

A pinched look furrowed Rowan's brow and he gave me a strained smile. "I try." He turned and walked back to the table he'd been sitting at before I'd barged in and I followed, taking the seat across from him.

"What are you reading?"

Rowan looked down and a small smile flitted across his mouth. "Ah—"

A laugh burst out of me when I saw the title. "*Dracula*, really? I've never read it but I can't imagine it's accurate."

"That's why I like it," he said, stroking one hand down the centre of the pages. "It's mostly long-winded descriptions and a little bit of mystery thrown in."

"Sounds... good?" I tried and smiled when he nodded distractedly. "Are you going to come with us this weekend?"

"To see the mage?" Rowan looked away from me, out into the stacks behind him so I couldn't read his face until he turned back to me. "I don't think so."

"Why not?"

He raised an eyebrow and it was the first time I'd really seen true irritation on his handsome face. "Because I think you're all idiots for going."

"That's why you should come," I needled. "It will be good to have someone there who doesn't think the trip is a good idea and can try and keep us in check." He looked unconvinced and I lowered my voice, looking up from under my lashes. "Please? For me?"

His eyes softened and the sigh that left him made him look deflated. "Fine, but I still think this is a terrible idea. You never know what you're going to get with a mage, they may work with us when the money is right but that doesn't mean they don't hate what we are. Unnatural. Damned."

"Do you really think that's true?" I hadn't given the spiritual ramifications of my transformation much thought, wasn't sure I believed there really were any.

He shrugged. "I believe that they think it's true."

"I'm not sure I ever had a soul to be damned in the first place," I mused and he shook his head.

"You have a soul, Leonora."

It felt like the case less and less these days. "Maybe," I murmured and a sigh escaped him.

"All I'm saying is... be careful, okay?"

"Always," I teased and pouted when he didn't smile back. But really, how could he take the word of a murder victim that they knew how to be careful?

Chapter Fourteen

"So you realise I don't have any money, right?"
I quipped to Hayes as I jogged to reach his side in the busy
corridor. He had class, I had a one-on-one meeting with
Elowen that had come as a surprise and I couldn't help but
feel concerned about whatever it was she wanted to say
to me.

"What?" Hayes said, looking at me sharply and I could
feel his confusion and irritation as clear as day through the
bond. *Great, it seems like it's only getting stronger.* "I assumed
you weren't talking to me."

"Why?"

"Judging by the hole in the wall where my door handle
hit it, thanks to you, I assumed that meant you were angry."

"Yes, well, nothing brings me as much joy as pissing you
off," I said sweetly, bright smile winking my fangs at him. His
eyes darkened to thunderstorm blue and I smirked.

"Why are you prattling on about money, love?" he said, a
sigh lacing his words that was at odds with the warmth I

could feel through the bond, making me squint at him suspiciously. *Love* was new too, but I tried not to read into it.

"The mage," I said quietly, "Rowan mentioned we would have to pay him."

Hayes' eyes narrowed and I wondered what I'd said wrong. "You don't need to worry about it. It's taken care of."

I raised an eyebrow. "What—" A cool breeze was my only response as Hayes decided he was done talking and ran off at incredible speed to his class. I was begrudgingly impressed. He was almost as fast as me, and that speed would only increase when he became a true undead.

A trickle of amusement came through the bond and I rolled my eyes as I rounded the corridor, ignoring the looks of anybody still milling the corridors as I headed towards Elowen's office. I hadn't been in there since I'd bitten her and I felt strangely nervous, like I was revisiting the scene of a crime.

The door opened as I approached and I halted at the entrance until Elowen called out for me to enter. Despite everything, I wasn't sure I'd ever get used to seeing magick used so casually.

"Please, have a seat." She gestured to the one in front of her desk with a delicately pale hand and I obeyed, feeling a strong sense of deja-vu calling back to my first night where I'd sat in this exact chair. "Do you know why I asked you here?" she said once I was sitting comfortably watching her.

I thought about it, biting my lip as I spoke slowly. "A lot of my first day as a vampire is a blur, but I remember Hayes saying that his job was to get me into the sanctuary discreetly. I wondered if this was because you knew something about how I came to be in the state I am, so close to Ashvale?"

Elowen watched me carefully, her cool face a blank mask

for whatever she was thinking at that moment. "Nothing quite so exciting," she said eventually. "I asked Hayes to be discreet as your appearance and circumstances were not that of the norm and I did not wish to alarm the other students."

"But how did you know where to find me if you knew nothing of my murder?"

A small smile made chills erupt on my skin as Elowen sat forward, resting her elbows on the hardwood desk. "I discovered the details of your death after the fact and sent Hayes to retrieve you. We have our own contacts for such cases—you didn't think we just sent our children out into the world without anyone to watch them at all? Watch," she clarified when I opened my mouth, "not intervene. What will be, will be."

Our children, she'd said. Did that mean Elowen had a child out there somewhere?

As if she could sense the questions brewing in my head, Elowen sighed. "I know nothing more than you about the circumstances surrounding your death, Leonora."

Lie.

I wasn't sure how I knew or what, exactly, told me as much, but in that moment I was certain that Elowen had just lied to me. She knew something, was actively *hiding* something, but I forced my expression to remain calm, remote. Whatever it was, I would find out—hopefully before it bit me in the arse.

"I called you here to discuss your magick," she continued, apparently satisfied that I had accepted her answer. "The ability to resist thrall is rare, and I feel that you would be better suited to exploring your abilities in our second year class."

I'd had no idea what to expect when I'd walked into her

office, hadn't even known what I was going to say to her until she'd asked the question and I'd really thought about it. But this? Magick lessons?

"When do I start?"

She smiled. "Tomorrow. You can walk to class with Hayes, he will introduce you to the instructor."

I nodded and, sensing I was dismissed, stood to leave.

"Leonora, before you go..."

I stopped at the door, raising an eyebrow.

"Please know that if you have any other concerns surrounding your transformation or arrival at Ashvale, you can and should come to me."

I nodded and smiled, like that wasn't more a threat than an offer of support and forced myself to stroll leisurely out of the office, only daring to speed up once I'd rounded the corner of the corridor and her office was out of sight.

I was panting as I ran, realising I hadn't breathed the whole time I was in there with Elowen. She may have wanted to appear friendly, innocuous even, but there was no mistaking my body's reaction to her. It went beyond fear. It was danger, the certainty of jaws about to close around your throat as you climb willingly into the monster's mouth.

I slowed my pace as I caught sight of Hayes in the grounds outside, completing what looked like hand-to-hand combat in a class of around forty. I'd instinctively followed the pull of the bond to him and I wasn't sure whether to be annoyed or relieved that my mind subconsciously equated him with safety.

He looked up at the window where I stood, like he could sense I was there watching and a strange curling sensation drifted through me, almost like a question. Had that been Hayes? He still stood, holding his sparring partner in a headlock seemingly effortlessly as he looked up at the window, at me, and the sensation came again.

I shivered and attempted an experimental stroke along the bond of my own, *reassurance*. I could talk to him about this later. Elowen might not to be trusted but I didn't think I was in any immediate danger.

Later then, I thought and saw Hayes nod like he'd heard as his sparring partner tried to twist free and he casually snapped his arm.

Stay safe, love.

CHAPTER FIFTEEN

IT WAS A GOOD THING I NO LONGER STRICTLY *needed* to sleep, because it had been evading me the more I tried to unravel my lost memories and my death. I found myself wandering the castle in the dead of night, enjoying the quiet and the touch of cool stone as the moonlight breeze toyed with my head through a cracked window. Normally, it was peaceful. But not tonight. I felt like I was floating above everything, taking the turns of my life with a nod and fanged smile without really processing it, and losing myself more and more in the process—or was I finding myself? Maybe whoever had killed me had done so because I was an absolute bastard. I had no way of knowing.

No, tonight the castle corridors and flickering candle light wasn't enough. I needed to breathe in the rain on the air and feel the dirt under my toes. I needed to feel *alive*, even if I was only pretending.

There was a small arched doorway at the back of the castle that I'd found during my night-time wanderings that led out right into the copse of trees beyond the sanctuary and its crumbling back wall. Why we hadn't come in this way the night Hayes had brought me here, I couldn't fathom Or, well, maybe I could—he'd probably done it to annoy me, to push me into confronting the changes of my body. Not that it did any good with the block in my mind, that whole night was a scramble of confusing emotions and warped memories.

The trees shuddered, short spiky branches trembling as the wind picked up before settling down. I could smell the clouds, as odd as it seemed, the heavy moisture was building and the air felt electric, like a tingle running over my body until I was the one shuddering.

There was a storm on its way, and as I walked further into the darkness between the trees I couldn't wait for it to arrive. The trees were strange here, some with thick and gnarled trunks and others were tall with cascading branches that reminded me of fir trees. They made me feel small as I walked beneath them, digging my toes into the dirt and not even feeling the stones or debris on the floor as I walked across it. There wasn't much light, but my heightened sight could see just fine and I hadn't realised how far I'd walked already when a small clearing opened up and I looked around with interest before freezing in place.

Shit. There it was again.

Silver fur gleamed as a long snout sniffed at the air in the brush on the opposite side of the open space. Any second now, it would realise I was here. It couldn't kill me though, right? I mean, how sharp could wolf teeth really be? I remembered the incredible speed the creature had moved with the other night and grimaced. Could I outrun it before it tried to rip my head off?

The wolf fell still, its nose to the ground, and then looked up abruptly, staring straight at me. Fuck.

For a second we just stared at each other, like neither of us quite knew what to do next. I probably smelled strange to the animal, and I wasn't sure what the limitations of my body were to know whether to fight or flee. I didn't really want to hurt it though, there was something all-too human in the stunning ice-blue of its eyes that made me hesitate.

I didn't feel fear, just wariness, which was strange. I thought I would be more concerned, given the size of the paws and the teeth I could see peeking out from the maw. Instead, I was...fascinated. I mean, it was certainly lethal, but also beautiful. Like a feral piece of moonlight roaming between the trees.

I placed one foot carefully behind me and the wolf watched me steadily, as intrigued by me as I was by it. I let my other foot move too until I was taking slow and steady steps away from the clearing and intro the relative safety of the trees. That was when the first paw fell forward.

I stilled, waiting to see what it would do next and a shuddering breath left me when the wolf took another step closer. Its nose raised to the sky and I thought it was going to howl but instead it chuffed at me before sinking back onto its haunches, ready to launch itself at me.

"Shit." Giving up on subtlety, I turned and fled, my eyes just barely keeping track of the trees and branches in my way before I could run into them at high speed—it would be too ironic to survive my murder, so to speak, only to accidentally stake my self running from a wolf I wasn't sure could kill me.

Except, it was fucking fast. I could hear its heavy paws thudding after me and the swift, panting breaths that came from its mouth as it growled. The sound chased me, bouncing from tree to tree in a rumble that made it feel like the forest was on the wolf's side, controlled by its whims.

Teeth nipped at my heels and I was actually a little tired by the time the half-fallen back wall that surrounded the castle came into view.

The wolf lingered amongst the treeline as I leapt over the small wall and landed in a crouch a brief sprint from the castle archway. I looked back at it and caught only the glimpse of long teeth glinting in the remainder of the moonlight.

I looked up in surprise. How long had I been in the forest for? The sky had begun to lighten and, while it wouldn't kill me, it would be annoying to have a sunburn if I stayed out here for too long.

I ran into the castle and threw a glance behind me at the last moment, wanting to make sure the wolf hadn't followed me in. Nothing. The woods were still. If it wasn't for the small snag in the fabric of my short nightgown, I might have thought I'd imagined the whole thing.

I stopped inside the archway and watched the forest from the window but didn't catch another glimpse of the wolf. I felt the dress at my back with my fingertips and traced the ragged outline of the claws that had ripped the material. It was close enough to shred my dress. It could have cut me, yet I remained unharmed. I shoved the encounter to the back of my mind as I moved away from the window and ran up the stairs towards my room. The strange wolf was a problem for another day—I had enough to worry about. Although, it had successfully distracted me from my own problems for a few hours.

I'd been so focused on getting back to my room and climbing into bed, that I hadn't realised somebody else was coming towards me until it was too late.

Strong arms caught me and familiar eyes widened in

shock as they took in the nightgown I'd thrown on before I'd gone out walking. I obviously hadn't expected to see anybody, let alone Rowan, and that was obvious from the length of the hem and the way it hugged my chest. I wasn't really sure I cared how indecent it was though, if they hadn't wanted me to wear it, then why leave it in my room?

"Leonora," he breathed and I steadied myself on his shoulders before pulling away.

"Sorry, I was lost in my head and wasn't paying attention." Elowen had been right, it was easy to lose track of your senses when you weren't concentrating. "Have you been out somewhere?"

He hesitated and then shook his head. "No, just in the library. Fell asleep reading," he said with a short laugh and I frowned. I could smell the outside on his clothes and the coming rain in his hair. Why lie? I supposed it wasn't really any of my business, it was just strange. But that was Ashvale all over: *strange*.

"Well, I'm heading to bed," I said and he nodded. "Sorry again for crashing into you."

"Don't worry about it. Hey, you'll be in West's class tomorrow right?"

I raised an eyebrow and he smiled, a slight blush rising to his cheeks. "Elowen mentioned it to me in passing when I had a meeting with her earlier today—I guess she's seen us hanging out together. I'll be in that class too."

"Second year magick, huh?" He nodded and I turned to face the end of the corridor where my room was waiting. "I guess I'll see you there."

"Sweet dreams," he murmured as I walked away and I couldn't stop the smile that curved my mouth as I unlocked my door and slipped inside.

CHAPTER SIXTEEN

WEST, THE INSTRUCTOR FOR SECOND YEAR MAGICK, was an undead vampire. The knowledge hit me instantly when I caught my first glimpse of him, a new wariness settling into me as I watched him, unsure how territorial he might be. So far, all I'd gleaned was that he was an insufferable arse.

Hayes choked at my side and I smirked.

"Some of us are fortunate enough to control an element, and occasionally these gifts run within the bloodline." West droned as he prowled up and down in front of the waiting class, all eyes fixed on him and the cane he gestured with. I could only assume it was a prop or a leave-over from his previous life, as a vampire wouldn't need it. Maybe it was just a statement piece, I thought as the bejewelled silver skull glistened in the light when he twirled it. I wasn't sure how long West had been an undead for, but he dressed like a nineteenth century gentleman, complete with a waistcoat, moustache, and pocket watch on a chain. Maybe he thought he was rocking the style—unfortunately, I couldn't agree.

"Others, like myself," he said smugly, the smirk on his face managing to look greasy despite his dry skin, "are powerful enough to be blessed with additional gifts too. Some of these you will be able to wield as a living vampire but others will be latent until you are undead."

He clearly wanted someone to ask, so I indulged him by raising my hand like a good little student. "What exactly are your powers, sir?"

West beamed and I stifled my irritation. I'd thought this class would be fun, instead it seemed to be a lot of sitting around and listening to West talk. "My element is fire," he said and when a ball of flames appeared in one of his hands he simultaneously bit into his wrist and let a small amount of blood flow.

"Magick, as all things in life, has a cost that must be paid. To conjure something from nothing, as one does with elemental magic, requires sacrifice. Blood, or something similar to pay the price, lest it bleed out of you in an uncontrolled manner."

That tickled something in the back of my brain, greying grass and ash in the air flashing into my mind's eye before vanishing and I frowned when I was unable to conjure the line of thought again.

"My other gift, one that uses my own well of energy and demands no other price but myself, is as a Searcher. It is what makes me so well-suited for life at the academy." He waited, but this time I didn't raise my hand and neither did anyone else. With a slight huff, he continued. "A Searcher can specialise in many things, for me it is power. I can look within you and sense what may slumber within."

Okay, that did sound kind of cool—but mostly because I wanted to know what kind of magick I had, *if* I had some, and not because I wanted to be a Searcher myself.

"As the majority of the class are still among the living, it is likely you will only be able to access or wield your elemental power for now. And be warned, not everyone will even have this much. Though, you may one day live long enough to accumulate the power to wield such energy."

It was fascinating to me how West could take a subject matter as interesting as literal fucking magick and make it boring. Hayes snickered quietly and West narrowed his eyes on us.

"Pair up!" he said abruptly and the room snapped to attention. "I want to see you summon your elements. As this is our first class together as part of your second year, I want to see where you're all at. Being able to summon your element quickly and controlled is of the utmost importance."

I stood to face Hayes and West was at our side in a blink.

"I think not, Miss Romilly. You have been a vampire for all of five minutes, as the kids say." His smile was more like a sneer as he instead grabbed Rowan from somewhere to his right and shoved him in front of Hayes. "You will watch. Next class I will assess your elemental reach."

He disappeared as quickly as he'd arrived and I scowled as I sat on the floor between Hayes and Rowan. "Come on then, boys. Show me what you've got."

A cocky smirk played on Hayes face as he lifted his hands and turned them inward, calling forth a perfect sphere of air that swirled in his arms before he dropped it.

"What price do you have to pay?" I asked, curious, and he glanced at me once before turning his eyes back to Rowan.

"Air is all around us, I don't have to summon it from nothing, therefore the cost is only personal."

"You take an energy hit," Rowan explained. "If you wield too much magick without sufficient energy, it could kill you."

Neat, I thought with a roll of my eyes. It felt like the things that could make me die a true death was an ever increasing list. "Now you," I demanded and Rowan laughed slightly.

He took up a pose similar to Hayes and held his palm out in front of him until a small orb of water flowed there.

"Water is also all around us, in the air, in the clouds," he shot me a look before adding, "in other bodies—so the cost for wielding this element is also lower, similar to Hayes. But if I tried to take too much in one go, the cost would be heavier and I would need to pay the price."

Interesting. So unless you wanted to be carrying around water or dirt or were prepared to bleed willy-nilly, then it was better to have an element like air that required less cost and less prep to wield. "Do either of you have extra powers?"

"No," Rowan said, a small frown marring his face. "Maybe when I'm an undead."

Hayes shrugged but I could feel his smugness radiating from the bond.

"Tell me what it is," I said and he pretended to think about it before offering me a taunting grin.

"No."

"You realise I could just ask the rest of the class right?" I'd seen a few people approach West during the session to be Searched and it seemed like a very public affair.

Hayes' mouth tipped up in a half-grin that mocked me. "As if I'd let West read me."

Fuck. There went that plan. "Tell me."

"No."

"Why not?" I whined and he prowled closer.

"What, so you can use it against me, love? I think bloody not."

"I'll find out eventually," I pointed out. Eternity was a long time to keep secrets.

"Then I suppose you're just going to have to wait."

Bastard.

~

"So you didn't even get to do any magick?" Novalie flipped through the genealogy book from the library as she sprawled on my bed and I groaned.

"Don't remind me." Apparently the first years had begun trying to find and wield their elements today, and I'd spent my supposedly more advanced class sitting on the sidelines.

"You know a little more than me about all this," I said, gesturing to the castle around us after a moment of silence that was broken only by the sound of pages turning. "Can I ask you something without you laughing at me?"

She sat up, eyes glittering with interest. "Of course. Spill."

"Are werewolves real?" I'd been mulling it over while I had been sitting through the tail-end of West's session and the more I thought about it, the more convinced I felt that there was more than met the eye when it came to the silver wolf. It had chased me when I'd run, though what predator would be able to resist the chase? But even then, it had felt more like...playing.

Novalie took the question seriously, her brows furrowing as she thought through whatever information she had stored away in her brain. "No," she said decisively. "Werewolves aren't a thing."

I wasn't sure why the answer disappointed me so much but when she continued on, the relief I felt was shocking.

"But vampire shifters do exist—it says it right here," she said, pointing to the genealogy book. "Some vampires can change form. "

I thought back to Rowan reading Dracula and nearly smiled. "Like a bat?"

"I guess? The most notable is the wolf—apparently the royals could all shift into a large wolf-like form. I think there have been some outliers throughout vampiric history, but the power to shift runs through the monarch line."

Could it be coincidence? What if my wolf was the missing heir? I wasn't sure how I could even check, I only knew that there had been something otherworldly about the wolf I'd seen twice now.

"Why do you ask?"

"Just curious," I murmured and she turned back to the book on the bed.

"There's a pretty comprehensive list in here of some of the gifts that run through lines, or extra gifts vampires have reportedly experienced. "

There was an excitement in her voice that was contagious and I couldn't help my smile. "Anything cool?"

"This guy," she said, handing the book to me as I walked over to sit next to her. "He could apparently fly."

"You could do that with the air element though," I pointed out and she nodded distractedly, already looking back through the book for more cool abilities to covet. "What about this one?" It was gruesome, but there was no doubt it could come in handy. "This girl could apparently cause people to implode."

"Gross." Novalie wrinkled her nose while I laughed. "How many times would you have exploded Hayes already if you had that power?"

I snorted. "I wish. The bond doesn't let us hurt each other. Not mortally anyway."

"Probably a good thing," Novalie said with a grin. "If killing each other is off the table you'll have to channel all that energy into something more practical."

I threw her a dirty look and she laughed harder. "You're lucky I can't explode you right now."

"Very," she agreed and we laughed again.

"Does anything run in your family line?" I asked as I flipped the pages and she looked surprised. "I mean, you don't need to tell me if you'd prefer not to."

"No," she said and then smiled a little. "I was just surprised you remembered. As far as I know, nothing runs in the family."

"I guess I'll have to wait and see if anything runs in mine."

"Do you remember anything about them? Your parents?"

I gave the question some serious consideration but shook my head. "Not really. I don't remember my dad at all, but my mum... I can remember her hair. I don't think she hugged me often, but when she did, I used to hold her hair in my tiny fist and marvel at it because it was so shiny and soft. I'd been jealous because my hair was curly and I wanted long, straight hair like hers."

Novalie smiled slightly. "Maybe you'll find her again one day."

"Maybe." Though I wasn't holding my breath that I would be claimed at the debut. But if I wasn't, it was fine. I could carve a place for myself out of this world if I had to, with enough room for Hayes by my side.

"You have the strangest look on your face right now," Novalie said thoughtfully and I smiled, letting more than a hint of fang show.

"Just thinking about burning the world down."

CHAPTER SEVENTEEN

I was supposed to be meeting up with Novalie, Hayes and Rowan in the late afternoon to head out to see the mage, but it was overcast and there was more grey fog than sunshine. I figured we could go a little earlier, potentially giving us more time to get there and back and also to stop at a shopping centre where I could pick out some clothes.

Hayes was on one of the upper floors somewhere, the throb in my chest tugging me in his direction when I suddenly spotted Rowan.

I didn't think I'd seen him since the night in the library where we'd almost... kissed? Bitten each other? I wasn't sure, but something about the way he'd neglected to mention it or seek me out since then made it feel like we'd done something wrong. Was it frowned upon for vampires to have more than one 'chosen'? Or was it just because Hayes had a history with him?

Rowan's face lit up when he saw me though, and I breathed a sigh of relief. I was glad I hadn't ruined whatever was between us, especially because I was worried about him. I frowned, realising it had slipped my mind that I'd actually seen him after the library—in the corridor after I'd run from the wolf, when he'd lied to me.

I squinted at him as he approached and his smile faltered slightly. "What? Do I have something on my face?"

"What?" I rearranged my expression and shook it off. "Oh. No! Sorry, I was just thinking about the other night. In the corridor?"

His face looked blank and then he nodded slowly. "Yeah, of course. What about it?"

Something about his response seemed strange, like he couldn't remember the encounter. "You were outside right?"

"Just a stroll," he said easily and I kept my smile in place even as my worry reignited. That wasn't what he'd said before and, unlike me, living vampires did need to actually sleep—so who went for a casual stroll at four in the morning? I'd have to mention it to Hayes, maybe he knew something I didn't about what was going on with Rowan.

For now, I would let it go.

"Listen," Rowan said, pulling me to a stop next to one of the alcoves in the wall. "You don't have to do this today. There are other techniques we could try first. Meditation. Hypnosis. I've been doing some reading and—"

"Well don't you two look cosy," a familiar voice remarked and a slight flush coloured Rowan's cheeks.

"Jealous, darling?" I smirked at Hayes as he leaned against the wall opposite, watching us with a frozen look in his eyes. "You should have seen us earlier," I taunted, leaning in close to Rowan so my lips were a hair's breadth from the pulse jumping in his throat. He swallowed hard and the wave of fury from Hayes made some part of me purr in satisfaction. I pulled back, not keen on inciting actual bloodshed between them. "We're going to see the mage, Rowan. If you don't want to come, then fine. But I don't want to waste my time meditating when the mage is more of a sure thing."

Promise of the bite fading, Rowan frowned but nodded. Hayes didn't look any happier as he stalked across the hall to capture my arm in his. "With me. Now."

Rowan's eyes widened and I threw him a helpless look as Hayes pulled me into one of the large, empty rooms that usually held classes on the first floor.

The door slammed hard behind us, the frame rattling in protest against the harsh treatment and I raised an eyebrow. "Something on your mind?"

His hand closed around my throat and I laughed, knowing he couldn't hurt me. Not truly. "Have you touched him?" The words were a snarl and I couldn't tell if his jealousy was over me or whatever he had shared with Rowan in the past.

"You mean like this?" I murmured, brushing my mouth against the underside of his sharp jaw, letting my breath feather across all the sensitive, sweet places that called to me. My fingers coasted down his chest and his breaths seemed uneven, a quiet growl escaping him when I dug my fingers in and then stroked away the sting.

"Or like this?" I moved my mouth up to his, our breath filling the space between our mouths as desire hovered in a fog that shuttered my brain for a second. I kissed him, parting his mouth with mine and claiming his tongue for my own, nipping and sucking and drinking his reactions in before I broke the kiss with a savage thrust to his chest. "No," I said eventually and there was a flash of relief on his face, softening his eyes, until I continued, "Not yet." Hayes scowled and I laughed. "If you want him, I won't get in the way."

His face was unfathomable, the bond strangely closed off all of a sudden as he watched me lean casually against the wall. "And if I want you?"

I blinked, unsure if he was being serious. *And if I want you?* Such an innocuous question, covering up so much more. "You don't," I said eventually and he was silent, just accepted my words like they held no importance. Maybe they didn't.

I loved to taunt him, liked to get as far under his skin as I could—and I knew he did the same thing to me. That was the beauty of knowing someone wouldn't ever leave. He could have my eternity, but giving him my heart? Well, he would need to work a lot harder for that.

An emotion I couldn't identify lit up his eyes and he relaxed as I wondered which of my thoughts he'd inadvertently picked up on.

"All of them," he replied, grinning when I scowled and I was thrown for a moment by the smile. I'd seen him smirk and taunt, but I wasn't sure I'd seen a real smile from him until now. It was... more breathtaking than I wanted to admit. Like the very air smiled with him.

"You're quite the romantic," he commented and I flipped him off as I turned for the door.

"Shut up. Let's go see a man about a murder."

IT WAS STRANGE TO BE OUT OF THE CASTLE, AND TO know that the last time I'd been truly out amongst humanity

I'd been alive. So much had changed in a relatively short period of time and it would only keep changing the longer I stayed undead, the more powerful I grew—and if I got my memories back... well, I wasn't sure who I'd be then.

It felt like the world should have changed somehow, too. I was dead. Fucking *dead,* and everything was the same, the world kept spinning. I was the one who was different and I was still working out if it was for the better. I had no idea who or what I might have left behind, who I might be missing or who might be missing me, and it was discomfiting to know someone out there might be worried, searching for me, mourning for me.

By the time we reached the mage's house I was more than ready to get back to Ashvale, if only so I could stop seeing what I was missing in the human world. It wasn't that I envied the humans, exactly, being a vampire was pretty fucking great. But having a choice in the matter would have been nice. I think that was what hurt me the most— watching humans and even the living vampires laughing, strolling around, taking all of that *choice* for granted. The journey had been strangely tense, or maybe that was just me. Rowan and Novalie had chattered on in the back seat while Hayes drove and I stared out of the window. He didn't attempt conversation, which I was grateful for. I wasn't sure I had the bandwidth to spar with him at that moment. Weirdly, just sitting silently next to him was comfort enough, and I suspected Hayes knew as much.

I'd been so busy mourning humanity as we drove that I hadn't given much thought as to what I expected from the mage—it wasn't *this,* though.

A regular house on a tiny street that was well-lit, almost cottage-like with a small green door and romantic grey brickwork. It was...normal. And so was the guy who answered Hayes' knock. I wondered a little belatedly how Hayes knew this person, but it was probably pointless of me to ask. Hayes was tighter-lipped than anyone else I knew, or, at least, as far as I could remember.

The mage was tall, with a dark mop of curly hair that covered the tops of his ears. Younger than I'd have imagined too. Of course, I wasn't necessarily picturing a long beard and a pointy hat, but the faded jeans and flannel shirt open over a grey tee just felt... weird. I was supposed to put my faith in this guy?

His light grey eyes widened slightly at the sight of us on his doorstep, but when they reached me he paled. Maybe it was a response I should get used to as an undead vampire, and one so young too, but I could only roll my eyes. He worked with vamps, he should be used to the shock value by now. I shot Hayes a glance, maybe this mage was actually about as useful and experienced as I was when it came to magick.

"Are you sure this is the right place?" I murmured and Hayes snorted as the mage stepped back and waved us inside.

"Unfortunately," the mage muttered and I raised an eyebrow as we walked inside.

"This is Cal," Hayes said over his shoulder, walking straight ahead and leading them into a sitting room that was surprisingly large. Wooden beams ran overhead and the exposed brick gave it a cosy, homely vibe that was nothing like I'd expected.

"Sorry, no cauldrons. I keep those in the kitchen," Cal said, deadpan as he scrubbed a hand over the dark stubble coating his chin and jaw while he watched us take in the space.

Hayes had clearly been here before and I couldn't help my shock at how comfortable he seemed in this man's presence, especially given how walled off he usually was. Hayes raised an eyebrow at me in challenge and I stalked over to him, sitting down next to him on the squishy leather sofa.

Rowan and Novalie shuffled in a little more hesitantly and took seats on the other two-seater sofa, leaving the armchair by the fireplace to the mage.

"What do you need?" Cal asked Hayes and I stiffened, not liking the sharp tone in his voice. Hayes seemed surprised too, so clearly this was not their standard interaction. Maybe he disliked that Hayes had brought us into his space, or, I reassessed as the mage's eyes flicked back to me, he wasn't keen on hosting an undead vampire.

"Problem?" I asked silkily and watched him swallow hard at the sound of my voice. "Don't worry, I'm sure your lack of hospitality is just because you don't keep much on hand for people like me."

Hayes sighed but I didn't care if he thought I was being rude. *Cal* had been rude to Hayes first. It wasn't my fault if the stupid fucking bond drove me to defend him.

"It's not necessary," Hayes said and I pointedly didn't look at him. If he wanted to have a conversation we could do it aloud, where he wasn't able to snoop on my bloody thoughts. "Well, stop thinking so loudly then," he hissed and I focused all my energy into imagining maiming him in the bloodiest, messiest way I could think of and was annoyed when he only laughed.

"As fascinating as this is to watch," the mage cut in, eyes keen on our interaction, "can we get to the point of this little visit?"

Hayes spoke over me, clearly knowing I was about to say

something unflattering. "Leonora needs help finding her memories. She was murdered before the block could naturally disperse and it locked her out of the memories of her mortal life."

The mage jolted slightly at the sound of my name and I watched him carefully for any signs of danger.

I told you that wasn't necessary, Hayes' voice drifted through me and my head whipped around as I smacked him on the arm.

"Stay out of my fucking head."

He bit his lip to suppress what I suspected was a laugh.

"I can kickstart your memories," the mage said, his brows coming together over his eyes in apparent concern that only put me on edge. "But it will hurt, and it will take time to come back fully."

"I don't have the time for that. Just give it to me in one go. I can handle the pain."

"Maybe," he said dismissively. "But if your mind was ready to process things then you would already be remembering." He looked at me askance and I stayed quiet. "Exactly. Forcing this is dangerous in itself, but making you remember *everything* here and now? Your mind could break. And the last thing we need is an insane undead vampire running around unchecked."

"Fine." I sighed. "Can we at least start with the most important memory? My murder?"

"What part of *'the trauma will drive you mad'* did you not grasp?" the mage snapped and I drew back, surprised.

"Cal," Hayes said reproachfully and the mage took a deep breath, turning away and walking out of the room to what I assumed was the kitchen judging by the sounds coming from that direction.

"I don't trust this," Rowan whispered, leaning from his seat to get closer to ours. "He doesn't seem like he knows what he's doing and if he does, well, he said it might drive you mad."

Novalie seemed a little concerned too but she just looked at me, waiting to see if I wanted to proceed. I nodded at her and she relaxed in her seat and resumed looking around the living space with undisguised interest.

"I have ears," I said blandly and heard Hayes snort.

"Maybe you're already mad," Rowan muttered and I shrugged. "I'm just trying to protect you," he insisted and I nodded slowly.

"I can take care of myself, thank you." My tone had been polite, but cool, and Rowan flinched.

Cal came back into the room and, thankfully, prevented Rowan from trying to talk me out of anything again. There was a slightly sweaty glass of bright purple liquid in his grip and I wrinkled my nose as I caught a whiff of it. "What is that?"

"Do you really want to know?" Cal said, a smirk on his mouth as he handed it over and I grimaced.

"No."

"Thought so."

"So I just drink this? That's it?"

He rolled his eyes and looked to Hayes as if to ask where he'd found me. "Drink it. I'll activate it. Then by the time you get back to Ashvale it will be starting to kick in."

"And what exactly will it do?" I said hesitantly as I sniffed delicately at the glass. It smelled like a mixture of blueberries and pickle and it looked *thick*.

"It will open your mind," he said and gave a meaningful glance to Hayes who nodded in response.

"Vague," I muttered and then downed the purple goop. "If this is poisonous I'll come back and haunt your arse."

Something like amusement glittered in Cal's eyes as he took the glass back from me.

"Noted." He looked to Hayes again and, fed up, I swivelled to face my bonded pain-in-the-arse. "Oh, sorry, are the secret looks just for you two?"

"Yes," Hayes said simply, and the smirk on his mouth made his red lips look annoyingly tempting.

"Whatever," I pouted and then stood. "Thanks for the juice. Let's get out of here."

"Appreciated," the mage said but there was a strange look on his face, a stark hunger, that had all my instincts screaming at me.

"Hayes said he would take care of payment," I said brightly and the mage laughed, the sound surprisingly rich. "I'll add it to his tab."

The sun had peeked out from the clouds when we stepped outside and I winced against the brightness. I was too young for the side effects other undead faced. That didn't mean I wanted to be out in it for longer than necessary though.

"Is it bothering you?" Rowan asked in concern. " Maybe the guy gave you some bad shit."

I raised an eyebrow, I wasn't sure I'd ever heard him swear before. "I'm fine, just a little prickly."

"I'll say," Novalie said with a laugh and I rolled my eyes in response even as I smiled. "Do you still want to go into town?"

"Yes." I was hoping to pick up a few things—namely, a night dress or other PJs that weren't shredded and ideally covered my arse a little better.

"Wait, what?" Hayes stopped in front of me and I swore as I nearly walked into the back of him again.

"We'll be quick," I promised. "I don't want to be out too long with this devil's juice rolling around inside me."

His gaze searched my face like he was gauging my sincerity before he nodded. "Fine."

After a few minutes of walking we found the right street and a sign for the shopping centre directed up to the left. Thankfully, the sunshine hadn't lasted long and the sticky heat was soothed by the strong breeze. Not that either particularly bothered me.

"Leah!" A deep voice called and I froze as it tickled at something in my mind. "Leah, wait!"

Hayes' hand gripped my elbow, in warning, but I turned anyway.

A young guy stood behind us, panting like he'd run down the street to catch up to me. He was tall and broad and the deepness of his skin seemed to shine in the daylight. I had no idea who he was.

"Holy shit," he said, eyes wide as he ran a hand over his close-buzzed head. "I can't believe it's you." And then I was in his arms. I tried not to stiffen, tried to let memory and sensation wash me away, but I couldn't do anything but stand there awkwardly until he let go. "Leah—"

"I'm sorry," I said gently. "I'm not sure who you are. I had an... accident. Amnesia."

His eyes grew even wider as I spoke. "Fuck."

"Yeah." Hayes and the others hung back but I could feel his attentiveness, his concern radiating like a beam of heat into my back.

"Um, well we actually don't know each other that well— I was just relieved you were okay. You never usually miss an appointment," he said, gesturing to my arms and after a second I realised he'd been indicating my tattoos.

"You did these?" I couldn't keep the surprise out of my voice, but he looked so... well, young. Not that I was one to talk, I supposed.

"Yeah, I hope you still like them, what with the..." He gestured to his head and I smiled slightly.

"They're beautiful. What was I supposed to come in for?"

"Knees," he said confidently. "You've been dying to get them done for months but wanted to wait until you had the cash."

My knees. I wanted to laugh at his small insight into who I was—am. If I wanted to get any other tattoos in the future I would need the help of a mage like Cal to alter my body.

"Well, we actually have to go," I said, gesturing vaguely behind me where the three living vampires waited, suddenly desperate to get away from the living reminder of the life I'd lost. "But it was nice seeing you."

"You too," he said and then shook his head. "Shit. I never even told you my name. Joel," He held out a hand and I took it before stepping back. "My shop is just up by Woking. Dragon's Heart. Come by any time. I'm only up this way visiting my parents."

"Was I local there too? In Woking?" The question flew out of me suddenly and Joel paused, clearly sensing it was important to me.

"You studied at one of the unis nearby," he said carefully and I nodded. So I wasn't local to the area around Ashvale then. Someone had either deliberately left me there or I had already been on my way somehow.

"Thanks," I said quietly, knowing I would probably never see him again. "Take care."

"You too."

My throat felt suspiciously tight as I walked back to the group of vampires and turned away from Haye's probing eyes. Suddenly, I wasn't so sure if I wanted to remember.

"You're too curious not to," Hayes said quietly and Novalie and Rowan moved ahead of us as we made our way into the centre of town and the shopping centre. "The only thing worse than knowing is not knowing," he finished and in a way, that made sense. Besides, I'd already drank the fucking purple goo.

"It will be okay," Hayes said, so quietly I almost thought I imagined it. Was he trying to *comfort* me?

Maybe hell was freezing over.

CHAPTER EIGHTEEN

I'D THOUGHT THAT VAMPIRES FOR DUMMIES WAS A boring class, but that was before I'd had to be lectured on etiquette by Lark. I'd waited for my memories to trickle back to me thanks to our visit to the mage at the weekend, but had only received a confusing jumble of dreams that left me crankier than usual.

"Your debut into vampiric society is perhaps one of the most important moments of your lives—undead or otherwise."

I managed to refrain from rolling my eyes—just. Yes, I was curious about my sire line and any abilities that might run in the family, but beyond that I thought the emphasis vampires placed on tradition just made them seem... Well, *old*.

"This is a special and fun occasion, but should also be taken seriously if you hope to encourage your sire line to claim you. Debuts happen once a year, so there will be a few second years and older students joining you as they missed the debut prior."

I almost dozed off, which was an impressive feat on Lark's part considering I didn't really need to sleep, but the sudden silence and pink flush to Lark's cheeks intrigued me enough to make me pay attention to his next words.

"I would be remiss not to warn you about some of the... other activities that often happen at these events." He cleared his throat and I watched in fascination as he flushed a deeper red. "As these events often involve bloodletting, the group of undead can sometimes influence the room subconsciously."

What on earth was he trying to say? At our blank faces, Lark sighed, rubbing the space between his brows for a moment. "Bloodlust is heightened in these situations where vampires congregate, as such things can tend to run a little... wild."

I wasn't sure what amused me more—the thought of stuffy, uptight vampires having a bloody orgy or Lark's embarrassment trying to warn us.

"Of course, you do not have to participate, but if you find yourself compelled by the rising bloodlust do not be alarmed, it's perfectly natural."

I couldn't hold my laugh in anymore and Lark jumped when it spilled out of me, his blush fading as he went pale at the sight of my fangs. It was ridiculous, really, how on edge some of the living vampires were around the undead, as if we weren't part of the same species. Sure, transitioning affected different vampires in unique ways. Some became less emotional, colder, others came into their own. I couldn't say which was true of me because I had no idea what I'd been like as a human.

"If you're quite done, Leonora," Lark said, frowning like he'd remembered he was supposed to be in charge. The way he said my name made my smile vanish. *Leahanura*. It was grating, but only because it echoed in my head long after he'd finished speaking, like a reverberation of the past rattling my head. Was this what Cal had meant when he'd said the purple drink would open my mind up to awakening the memories? That I'd get a fat bloody headache?

I stood slowly and Lark took a step back before catching himself. "I need to be excused."

He nodded, relief breaking across his face as I made for the door. Clearly he was just happy I wasn't tearing out his throat. I didn't have the energy to find it funny right then. I could barely think past the pain in my head, like I had a knife piercing me through my temple and poking at my brain.

Hayes. I needed Hayes.

LIke he'd heard me or maybe had just felt my pain, he appeared around the corner I was walking towards and I swayed, catching myself on the wall. "What's happening?" I said through gritted teeth and Hayes frowned, his jaw tight as he took my weight against him and manoeuvred us up the stairs to the third floor.

"I'm not sure. I'll call Cal."

I nodded, barely breathing to try and reduce the miniscule movements of my body that set my head throbbing worse than before.

Hayes swore but I couldn't tell why because my eyes had slid closed. Warm hands slid under my knees and then I was weightless as he carried me to my room, his sweet scent enveloping me until my head lolled against his chest, content.

I didn't remember him putting me to bed, but that's where I found myself when I opened my eyes, his voice a dark hum as he spoke to someone on the phone.

"What the hell did you put in that stuff? She practically collapsed in my arms, Cal."

The mage. I was too tired to move, so I stayed still and just listened, the concern and anger in Hayes' voice surprising me as he continued to chew out the mage over the phone. I only realised he was sitting next to me when his hand sank into my hair, stroking the long strands out in a gentle tugging motion that made me want to purr. I doubted he would continue if he knew I was awake, though.

"Well, you need to fucking fix it."

I concentrated and could hear the other side of the conversation without my head hurting worse. "I didn't do anything wrong, Hayes. Her trauma or the remnants of the block are what's causing her problem. Just..." I listened intently, eager to hear what the mage would say next. A deep sigh sounded over the line. "Just sit with her. Okay? Take care of her—you might even be able to take some of her pain through the bond."

So my head was more fucked than we'd thought. It explained why nothing had really happened over the weekend after we'd come back from the mage's house.

I let my eyes flutter, I'd heard enough.

"She's waking up. I'll keep you updated." Hayes' hand stilled on my hair, like he hadn't realised what he'd been doing, or maybe he just wasn't sure if I wanted his touch. "How are you feeling?"

"Still hurts," I rasped and licked my lips. "But not as bad."

"Were you doing something that could have brought it on?"

"No, I was just—" I frowned. "Well, I was thinking about how Lark says my name and how it sounded similar to the accent of the tattoo artist from Saturday. Joel."

Hayes nodded, a look of relief flashing across his face as I sat up by myself. "Maybe it was close to triggering a memory."

Now I understood why Cal had said the pain and trauma might drive me mad.

I licked my lips again, my throat feeling uncomfortably dry, and nearly jumped when Hayes snuck an arm around my waist and lifted me with ease onto his lap.

His eyes were intent on mine and he was all I could see, my vision consumed by the depth of blue. I swallowed. "What are you doing?"

His hand traced lazy circles into my back and it felt good. Really good. And that was the problem.

"You need this," he said quietly, like he knew I would hate to have my vulnerabilities spoken aloud. "Let me do this for you."

He tilted his head one side and I settled my legs around his hips when his forehead hit my shoulder. It was a twisted embrace, I mused, as I nuzzled my face into the crook of his neck and inhaled deeply. The truth was, he made my mouth water from more than one kind of hunger.

I sank my teeth into him in a slow glide that had his hands tightening on my waist. Blood hit my tongue and I relaxed at the first taste, sweet and rich, comforting even as heat moved through me, flowing down the bond and into Hayes.

I shifted in his lap restlessly and he stilled me with a tightening of his hands on my hips, his groan was low and breathless. "If you want me to stay in control then you need to stop moving like that, love."

The thing was, I wasn't sure I *did* want him to stay in control. I pulled from him deeply and the answering shift of our bodies couldn't be resisted, the desperate arch of my back and the slow slide of his hands down my body to capture the backs of my thighs as he encouraged my legs to move wider felt inevitable.

I could feel him, hard and growing harder beneath my hips, and when I pulled back and licked his wound shut, we stared at each other for a breathless moment before I tilted my own head in offering and he gave in with a growl that set my body humming.

His bite was clean, deep, and the hand that reached up to cradle my head massaged it as he fisted my hair. My hips rolled and his other hand moved to grip the full roundedness of it tightly—not to stop, but to encourage.

More.

I wasn't sure which of us had thought it, but I couldn't deny I wanted it. Wanted everything.

Hayes pulled away from my throat long enough to pull my fitted black tee up and off over my head, blood trickling down from the open wound until it ran between my breasts. His mouth followed it hungrily, licking a line of fire across my chest as he made deft work of my bra.

This was spiralling out of control and I couldn't bring myself to care. Too lost in his taste, in his smell, in the scorching heat of his palms as they cupped my breasts, stroking my nipples with his thumbs as he looked down at my soft curves with a hunger that might have made me blush if I was still human.

I wanted to feel more of him, his flesh under my fingertips, but he was too busy to let me get my fill. Warm lips ghosted over me, licking and tasting until his tongue curled around my nipple and I gasped, my head tipping backward as he feasted on me. A quick sting made me look down and Hayes looked up at me, his fangs glistening and his eyes nearly black as his pupil swallowed the iris. A fresh puncture wound was on my breast and when he lowered his head to drink I cried out at the sharp pain mixed with a heady pleasure that made me desperate to remove the final layers of clothing between us.

Hayes didn't seem inclined to move and I growled as I grabbed his face, pulling it up to mine and kissing it savagely, tongues and teeth colliding in a biting kiss that left us both panting. I ripped his shirt in my effort to get it off as soon as possible and he looked bemused as the tatters of it hung around his body.

The space between us evaporated as his hands found my zipper, tugging my jeans down roughly until they hung open at my hips, revealing the fragile black lace covering me as I spilled out of the seams. His hands stroked down my waist reverently, squeezing my arse, barely covered by the lace before he shuddered. "Off. Now."

I stood and immediately hated the distance between us as I pulled my jeans the rest of the way off and let my underwear follow suit.

There was the thinnest band of blue visible in Hayes' eyes as he took in my curves, the fullness of my breasts, hips and thighs, and the softness of my belly.

His jeans hit the floor and I blinked, barely having seen him move. I hid my smug smile. He was coming undone, and it was because of *me*.

"Of course it fucking is," he growled as he strode to me with purposeful movements that spoke of domination. "You drive me fucking insane, Leonora."

His mouth claimed mine and his chest brushed against

me before he lifted me and I hooked my thighs around his hips.

I groaned as his mouth found my neck again, trailing kisses there before he licked tauntingly at the small puncture wounds on my neck and then my breast.

He looked up, glancing at the distance between the wall versus the bed before backing up and letting me stay atop him as his thighs flexed beneath me.

I took the hard length of him in my hand and stroked him as his tip rested against my entrance.

His eyes fluttered closed as his head fell back, exposing the long, strong column of his throat, smeared with blood— his or mine, I couldn't say.

"Leonora," he panted and I revelled at the sound of my name on his tongue. "Stop fucking teasing and *ride me*."

I obeyed, sinking down onto him hard, and we shuddered in sync as the bond seemed to flare inside of us. I rolled my hips and nearly came straight away as my pleasure redoubled through his, the connection making every sensation a beautiful torture. "Shit."

Hayes' jaw was clenched tight as he fought for the same control I needed too. "I think we're going to have to go hard, love. Because if you don't move soon, you might kill the both of us."

I obeyed, lifting my hips up and slamming them down, aching for him to fill me and gasping when he did, his dick driving in and sending me pulsing. Slick wetness formed between us as I moved desperately, building us into a fever pitch of movement. God, it was like I'd started coming when we were joined and I hadn't stopped. Small sparks made my breath ragged as Hayes took over, pulling me to his chest and thrusting up into my pussy, moaning into my ear as he found an angle that drove the both of us wild. "You're dripping for me, love. Do you hear it? Can you hear how much you want me?"

My voice was overtaken by moans as I begged him with my body for release. "Oh, oh, oh—don't fucking stop you bastard."

His chuckle rumbled through me as he stilled, sitting me back up on top of him so he could take my wrist in his hand. I immediately set a furious pace, my hips rocking hard into his until his smug smile disappeared, replaced by one of intense hunger.

He bit cleanly into my wrist and the pull of his mouth and sting of his teeth sent me over the edge. I clamped down around his dick and he moaned around my skin, meeting me thrust for thrust until we both cried out.

He sat up, letting my wrist fall between us, my blood smearing across his muscled chest as he pushed us harder.

Our bodies pressed together tightly, his heat bleeding into me as his hand slid under my thighs, lifting them slightly as he moved with a ferocity that had us both shattering with a cry of bliss that bordered on pain.

I wasn't sure what sex had been like as a human, but I had no doubt that it hadn't been anything like what we'd just experienced—especially with the bond taking his pleasure and running it through me and vice versa.

Hayes pressed a kiss to my shoulder and despite myself, I felt relaxed, safe in his arms as he cradled me, stroking lazy fingertips over my spine as he laid back against the bed without jostling me.

"That was—"

"Inevitable," I supplied and felt him nod.

"How's your head?"

"Fine," I said, surprised that it was true. I wasn't sure if it was something about the magick of the bond, healing me in ways I couldn't understand, or if it was just getting my mind off of the memories trying to break their way through and instead going blissfully blank with pleasure.

"Good," he said quietly and I hid my smile in his chest.

Chapter Nineteen

The bite marks on Hayes' throat were obvious, still rimmed in a little bit of red as they healed. As the other half of my bond, it wasn't surprising the thrill I got from seeing them on him—or, rather, knowing that everyone else could see them and know he was mine. But it was the fact that Hayes displayed them almost proudly that stroked my ego.

I would miss them when they healed—probably by the end of the day, if not sooner.

The four of us sat in the library, reading books on meditation to see if we could bring on my memoires in a slightly less painful way, and Rowan kept sneaking glimpses at me and Hayes alternately until I sighed and slammed my book shut.

"Do you have a question?"

Novalie looked intrigued, sitting forward from her place in the middle of the wooden tables, her skirt fanned around her. Rowan looked up and then away. "No."

"I do," Novalie said chirpily and I snorted.

"Well, when an undead vampire and a living vampire like each other very much—"

Novalie laughed and Hayes rolled his eyes, but not before I saw the small smile on his lips. Rowan didn't react, just continued reading like we didn't exist and I sighed. When had things become so messy?

"I don't recall a time when things weren't messy," Hayes said and Rowan's head shot up.

"It's rude to have a mental conversation in front of those of us who can only hear one side," he chided and Hayes raised an eyebrow.

"Why don't we try to wake a memory?" Novalie cut in, and I shot her a grateful look. There seemed to be more and more tension between Hayes and Rowan lately, and it seemed like I was the cause. I stood and hopped up onto the table, sitting down cross-legged opposite Novalie. She took my hands in hers, which were surprisingly soft, and I smiled. My hands had callouses—from what, I obviously didn't know, but clearly I'd worked hard at something for it to have left evidence on my skin.

"Okay, the book says you should focus on an emotion— just one, to prompt the memory, something that will be associated with that feeling." I nodded and Novalie continued, "What do you want to start with?"

My instinct was to say fear, so I could finally get some answers about what had happened to me and who had done it, but after the headache I'd had before, I felt like I should be careful to heed Cal's warning.

"Humour," Hayes suggested and I relaxed. Yes, humour was a good one.

"Okay. Clear your mind. Focus on your breaths—" She seemed to realise at that moment that technically I didn't have natural breaths. "Um, focus on Hayes' breaths," she suggested instead and I nodded, tuning into the beat of his heart and the whoosh of his lungs as my mind emptied, calmed.

"Good, now let's focus on the emotion. What do you find funny, how does it make you feel? Sink into the feeling of it and let your mind cast you back. Don't fight it."

I did as she instructed, my body growing pleasantly warm and I could almost feel the ghost of my heartbeat as I focused.

It was almost like dreaming. A girl appeared. She had bright red hair and a piercing above her lip, her laugh was infectious and she kept going until she was crying with it, her slim shoulders shaking. I couldn't see anybody else, just her, and I had no idea what we had been laughing at, but I was certain that whoever she was, she'd been my friend.

"Did you see something?" Rowan asked, standing up and peering into my eyes when they opened.

"A girl," I murmured. "We were laughing. I think she was my friend."

"So now you just need to remember something useful and maybe it'll be like dominos, coming back one after the other."

"Maybe," I allowed and she smiled. "To be honest, it was draining just remembering that small snippet." I was a little concerned about my hunger getting the better of me if I continued opening memories one-by-one like this.

"Let's get out of here then," Novalie said, flinging her book down onto a pile. "I'm starving, anyway." I hid my smile. Novalie always seemed to be starving.

"I could eat," Hayes said, surprising me. "You coming Rowan?"

"Sure," he said, whatever tension lingered between them dissipating easily. The space between the stacks seemed a little too tight for all four of us as we left, the pages of books fluttering in the breeze of our passage.

"I appreciate you guys helping me with this," I said as we neared the door that led back out into the corridor.

Novalie grinned as she taunted me. "Aw, Leonora, are you being sentimental?"

I didn't reply, too distracted by the smell drifting towards us. It hit my keener senses first, and then the others moments later.

Blood. And it was fresh.

I could hear footsteps behind me as I ran towards the smell, stomach churning as I drew closer. Surprisingly, the scent did nothing for me, perhaps because I just *knew* that what we were about to see wasn't going to be anything as pleasant as a standard feeding—hell, I would have taken a blood orgy at that point.

A figure stood not too far ahead of me and I stopped moving to watch them. They were a dark silhouette until they shifted slightly and the dim candle light illuminated his face.

It was a living vampire, not one I particularly knew, but I'd seen him around. He was one of those that often stared at me like they were seconds away from slitting their wrists and offering themselves up, just for the chance at power.

But the source of the heavy metallic scent was the girl being held against the wall, her head lolling awkwardly as the living vampire continued to feed. He was taking too much.

"Hey!" I'd seen enough. I moved forward, my new speed bringing me to him in mere breaths, but instead of his usual fear or awe, there was only a feral creature staring back at me.

He snarled low in his throat and, even if he hadn't been about to kill what I could smell was a human, my vampiric side was not going to let an insult like that stand.

Hayes was the first to reach us, with Novalie and Rowan not far behind, but they were still too late to try and stop me. The crack of the living vampire's neck sounded out before they'd stopped moving.

I dropped him dispassionately and moved towards the girl. She was Black, pretty and her hair was braided into spirals across her head that would have been stunning if so much of her wasn't painted red. The rich hue of her skin was faded to an unnatural chalkiness but I could hear the very faint beat of her heart. I focused on that, on her, as I bit my wrist and pressed it to her mouth.

Was this what I had looked like? When the vampire had killed me? More blood than person? Just meat that had been discarded?

One of the group had clearly left to retrieve Elowen, but I'd been too focused on the girl to notice their departure or her arrival.

Her steps faltered on the floor as she took in the scene, a cold word escaping her. "Explain."

Rowan spoke to her quietly as I continued funnelling my blood into the girl. I could only hope it would heal her enough—I was young, and typically the older, more powerful the vampire, the easier it was to heal grave wounds. Both your own and others. I wasn't even a month old, there was no way this should be working, but her heart was definitely beating stronger. Suddenly, it stopped and I looked down in alarm. At some point I'd pulled the girl onto my lap, heedless of the blood, to continue feeding her in a more dignified pose. She wasn't just something to be used and discarded. God, had I killed her?

In a sense, Hayes thought and I looked up at him blearily, confused, rage burning through me.

"Leave the girl, Leonora."

I stood so quickly I knew I must have been a blur to the others. Not Elowen though, her eyes remained on me the whole time. "Is that all you have to say? One of your students brought this girl here and nearly killed her."

Her head tilted to the side as she watched me. "And you killed him."

"Not yet," I said, looking at the place where the living vampire lay, his body repairing itself as he prepared to make the transition to an undead. "What, exactly, are you going to do about this?"

There was something of a challenge in Elowen's stare that should have frightened me, but I couldn't feel anything past the rage that threatened to send me over the edge.

"Well, I believe all of the appropriate measures have already been taken," she said finally and my body tensed. "The culprit has died his first death, and the girl is alive. Or, rather, undead."

"What?" My lips felt numb as I turned to see the girl blinking on the floor where I'd left her as the wound on her neck closed over. She was still far too pale, but she was alive. Wasn't she?

Elowen took advantage of my momentary distraction and approached to murmur in my ear. "It shouldn't be possible. The girl should be dead. To turn through bite or blood often ends in failure, even when the vampire in question is hundreds of years old."

I didn't know what to make of her words. They sounded

like a warning, a threat, but her face was blank even as her eyes gleamed with a strange light. "For better or worse, she is your responsibility now." Elowen made to step towards the living vampire, now undead, her skirts swirling around her ankles in a mist of black but I shook my head.

"Leave him." It was a command, I realised belatedly, and from the way Elowen stiffened, she didn't appreciate it any more than my vampire-side would have. "Please," I added, a slight peace offering, but she did as I'd asked and that was all that mattered really. Vampires understood the need for violence, especially when it came to retribution—nobody more so than the undead.

Hayes raised an eyebrow at me and I nodded, knowing what he was asking. I approached the girl who was beginning to stir and ignored the groan of the vampire I'd killed as Hayes hauled him up.

"What are you going to do with him?" Rowan asked and I flicked him a quick glance.

"For now, we're just going to hold him." It hadn't escaped my notice how his voice had gone up at the end of the question, like he feared what I would do, what I might become.

Eyes fluttered open to reveal dark irises and I smiled as comfortingly as I could. "Hello. I'm Leonora, what's your name?"

"Emerson," she said, and then touched her mouth as if surprised she'd replied. "Why did I tell you that?"

"I'll explain everything," I soothed. "But first, I need your help. Okay?"

Emerson hesitated and then nodded slowly, warily. Smart girl.

"This man," my lip curled at the word, as if it were an

even slightly accurate depiction of the slimy prick who'd done this. "This man tried to hurt you, and in order to save you, I ended up turning you into something like me." Her eyes were wide, but she was listening. Good. I flashed her my fangs and she inhaled a sharp breath of air. Fear. "Now, you can either join us or you can choose to let go."

"Let go?"

I hesitated but decided to just come clean with it. "You didn't survive the attack, Emerson. You can either live your new life as a vampire, with us, or you can die. The choice is yours. I'm sorry there wasn't time for me to save you properly."

Her mouth opened and closed before she settled on, "That's the man who attacked me?"

"Man is a bit of a strong word," I muttered, following her eyes to the vampire in question. "But yes."

"What happened to him?" she asked as the vampire groaned again.

"I killed him." Her head whipped back to mine as she scooched further away. "For killing you," I added and that eased some of the suspicion on her face. "I wish you had more time to process this, but you need to decide now, before bloodlust kicks in and you... well, you won't like the results and you'll die anyway."

"I want to live," she whispered and my shoulders eased, relief filling me. I wasn't sure why I cared so much, only that I did. Maybe I saw something of myself in her, in our shared trauma.

"Your heart won't beat," I said and she watched me speak with an intent look on her face. "But neither will his."

There. Flashing in her eyes. I smiled. Emerson was a fighter, she belonged here. WIth me.

With us, Hayes corrected and I shot him a scowl over my shoulder.

"One last question." I helped Emerson to her feet. "Do you want to kill him or shall I?"

Rowan stepped forward. "Leonora—" I ignored the alarm in his voice.

"He's yours if you want him. He won't come back this time. But if you're not sure then—"

Emerson was already shaking her head. "I'm-I'm not ready for that."

"Then will you allow me the honour?"

"Yes please," she whispered and my lips curved as I turned to the vampire I'd already killed once.

"I have a question." His eyes snapped open and there was fear on his face as he watched me move closer. He struggled in Hayes' arms but quickly stopped when he realised how weak he was. "I find it very interesting that there's now two girls who have been bitten and drained within the same month." He struggled harder and I stepped closer, blinking in surprise when Hayes seemed to pull a blade out of nowhere and hand it to me. "Decapitation is so messy," I said, sighing as I pretended to consider my options. "Tell me. Did you kill me?" I put as much power behind the command as I could, focusing on the living vampire with everything I had and his eyes widened even as he stopped struggling, perfectly held in thrall before he shook his head.

I gave a sharp nod of acknowledgement and relief filled his expression as I dropped the knife from where I'd held it to his throat, only for fear to find him again as I moved quickly, thrusting the blade into his chest.

"Found the heart on the first try," Hayes said and I was

glad there was nothing but respect on his face. I knew if I turned to Rowan I wouldn't be able to say the same thing.

I let the vampire's corpse fall to the floor and stepped over him, leaving him there the same way he would have left Emerson. The way somebody like him had left me.

"Let's go to bed," I muttered, suddenly beyond tired. "Emerson, you can stay with me until we get a room sorted for you." I linked her arm securely in mine and didn't look back as we left the vampire who killed her on the floor in the middle of the corridor.

Chapter Twenty

"I'm not sure I know who I am anymore," I murmured to Hayes the next morning. Elowen had sent one of her lackeys over to collect Emerson about half-hour ago, and I'd been hesitant to let her go with them. After all, the last time she'd been alone with a living vampire she'd died.

In the end, it was Emerson who'd convinced me she'd be okay. Apparently Elowen needed to smooth things over with the authorities and anyone important in Emerson's life now that she was dead—which made sense really and only emphasised how much I still had to learn.

"You're Leonora Romilly," he said after a second, looking over at me from where he'd made himself comfortable on my side of the bed, his arms behind his head as he sprawled. "Pain in my arse. You're you," he said as I laughed quietly. "You're special."

"What if I don't want to be?"

He shrugged and rolled onto his side to face me. "Tough."

I snorted. "There seems to be more shit every day that I

can do that I'm not supposed to be able to... What if something's wrong with me? What if something went wrong during the transformation and I'm some kind of... anomaly."

He smiled, just a small quirk of his lips but I caught it anyway. "There's nothing wrong with you. You're just—"

"Yeah, yeah, special. I heard you before." I sighed and rolled onto my back, away from his knowing gaze until I couldn't take it anymore. "What?" I snapped and he chuckled.

"I think you do like it. Being special, I mean. Who wants to be just like everyone else? And look at you—you've clearly never been anxious to fit into a crowd, otherwise why get all the tattoos? I don't see any reason why you should change that now."

I shrugged. "That was the old me though."

"The old you is no different from undead you." At my disbelieving look he snorted. "Okay, yes, there are a few differences, but I don't believe your personality could have changed that much. You care deeply about people and justice, and you're bold." He cleared his throat and I watched, fascinated. I wasn't sure I'd ever seen Hayes embarrassed before. "Plus, nobody is naturally as good in bed as you are. Some things just stick with you."

I laughed and after a second he joined in.

"Did I hear laughter coming from this room or do my ears deceive me?" Novalie called as she walked in uninvited. "Aw look at you two. Next, you'll be plaiting each other's hair and singing *kumbaya* around a fire."

I rolled my eyes but Hayes' expression had already shuttered. *Why do you do that?* I wondered and knew he'd heard and chosen not to answer when a muscle in his jaw ticked.

"I'll leave you guys to talk," he said as he swung up from the bed and was halfway to the door before I had even opened my mouth. "I'll see you in class later."

Novalie watched him go, looking as bemused as I felt. "Was it something I said?"

I shrugged. "He's testy."

"Yet, you've wormed your way into his heart anyway."

"Heart? No. Pants? Yes."

Novalie snorted and I patted Haye's vacant spot on the bed. "How are you doing with everything? Like, does it bother you? Me and Hayes?"

She shrugged. "You know, not as much as I thought it would, to be honest."

"I'm glad," I said and raised my eyebrows when she looked at me sceptically. "I mean it. I like you and I wouldn't want to hurt you—but there's not much I can do about the bond with Hayes."

"I know," she said and the silence that fell between us was comfortable. "Besides, I've kind of been talking to someone else."

"Oh?" I wondered if it was Rowan but I couldn't see them together, really. Novalie was... Fun. Impulsive. Rowan was more inclined to stay on the safe side, controlled, quiet. That was fine, it was even sexy at times, but I couldn't see them actually getting together beyond a hook-up, maybe.

"Yeah, there's that girl in our classes with Lark—dark hair and eyes, Siera?"

"I think I know who you mean, she's pretty."

"I know right." Novalie sighed dreamily and I grinned. "Do you think you'd ever date a girl?"

"Do I need to let Hayes know he has competition?" I teased and we laughed. "I don't know—I've never really been into girls, but that doesn't mean I definitely wouldn't. I think it's more about finding the right person. Plus, eternity is a long time to never touch a boob I guess."

We laughed and continued chatting until I checked the time and groaned. It was time to be tortured by West.

"With any luck I might actually get to do some magick this time," I grumbled to her and she patted my shoulder sympathetically.

"I've got my fingers and toes crossed for you."

Unfortunately, I was pretty sure I was going to need all the luck I could get.

I made my way to the same room I'd seen West in before and found the majority of the class already there. West frowned at me as I strode in and I opted to ignore him, not wanting to start any kind of pissing contest—not when I was hoping he'd read me today.

I found Rowan and Hayes sitting in the third row back on a nearly-empty long table. A few stares lingered on me as I walked in which I found odd. Most people were used to seeing me by now and didn't take much note of my presence. What was different about today?

"Word travels quickly," Hayes said as I sat down. "Some people are.... unhappy, about what happened to Colin."

I raised an eyebrow and Rowan frowned.

"The living vampire you killed," Rowan said, more than a hint of accusation in his tone when he added, "Twice."

I grimaced. His name had been Colin? "Well, I guess there's a reason you don't often hear about vampires named *Colin*."

Hayes coughed to hide a laugh but a living vampire in the row ahead of us shot me a glare that I returned with a wide smile. He looked away at the sight of my fangs and I relaxed back into my seat as West cleared his throat.

"Those of you who have yet to be read by a Searcher, please line up before me."

Everything about his tone was begrudging, but I could see the gleam in his eye even from my seat near the back. He may not want to help us come into our power, but he *did* like showing off his own.

I stood and walked towards the front of the room with a handful of others, all living vampires. One girl tried to elbow me to get ahead in the line and I caught her arm before it could dig into my ribs, snapping it effortlessly and continuing on like nothing had happened as she cursed up a storm behind me.

They could be mad about the death of *Colin* if they wanted, but I didn't regret it. He had murdered Emerson and who knew how many others. I'd done what was necessary. If I had to break a few bones to drive that point home then I would, happily.

West paused in front of the first vampire in the queue and held his hand to the side of the vampire's head. A faint warmth seemed to come from between his palms and I watched in as much fascination as everyone else in the class as a small glow appeared between his fingers.

West took a step back, nodding as he declared, "Air!" and then waved the living vampire away. Clearly the elemental magick was unimpressive to him, but I thought *any* magick was fucking cool.

The next guy in front of me stepped forward eagerly and West received him with a look of boredom on his face, placing his hands at the man's temples the same as before. Warmth, then light, and West looked slightly less disinterested as he stepped back. "Flame. I can sense something else within you, but I will have to go deeper." He barely waited for the living vampire to nod before placing his hands against the living vampire's head once more. The glow and heat seemed more powerful this time, like West was channelling more than before, and after a second objects around the room began to float in the air—a chair, a bag, and several books, before West broke the connection and the items fell back to their positions with a thump. "Telekinesis."

The living vampire seemed pleased but West was too distracted by the next face in line to pay him much attention. Mine. "Elowen believes you have some kind of natural resistance to enthrallment."

I nodded as I stepped forward. "Yes."

"But you're hoping for more than that."

I shrugged. "Who wouldn't?"

A small smile ghosted across West's face and I narrowed my eyes.I didn't like the look on his face—not one bit.

He stepped forward and his smile widened when I instinctively tensed. "Let's see what you're really made of," he said quietly and I stared stubbornly back, unsure why he seemed to have such a problem with me. But some members of the undead were just like that—territorial.

His cold hands cupped my face, his fingertips resting at my temples, and I could feel his mind brushing against mine, probing and searching. The gentle warmth of his power began to heat up alarmingly fast and I wondered if this was how it had been for everyone else, if this was all part of the process, or whether he was trying to harm me. My eyes flashed open but West's stayed shut. His whole body stiffened and his eyes roamed beneath his lids, body spasming occasionally.

I tried to turn my head, to find Hayes, but it was held firmly in place as West's grip tightened.

I gasped as the heat seemed to sear into my skin and I was surprised when it didn't bubble right off. West's eyes snapped open, wild and distant like he was seeing something I couldn't. A pale hand gripped West's arm, trying to pry it away from me without success, and it was clear that West was no longer in control.

"What are you?" he whispered and as the room darkened, I felt real, true, fear for the first time since becoming a vampire. Thunder rumbled in the distance and the hair on my arms and West's head stood straight up as the tangy scent of ozone filled the air. Wind began to swirl around us, whipping my hair about with a ferocity that felt as freeing as it did concerning. It was like being caught in the centre of the storm. A surge of power charged the air between us and lightning struck just out of my periphery once, twice, three times, the bright light just a smear of white in the corner of my eyes. If there were sounds of alarm, I couldn't hear them past the wind in my ears.

I wasn't sure if this was West's doing or mine, but neither of us had control over it. West's hands shook as they released me and he dropped to his knees, eyes rolling up into his head as he trembled like he'd touched a livewire.

Leonora. It was Hayes, his voice laced with a panic that surprised me as another wave of static-electric power rose in the room, like a tide waiting to sweep everyone away. It cut off Hayes' words and I drowned in the power that seemed to pulling from me like a conduit.

You need to turn it off, his voice came through again but I didn't know what to do—if this was really my doing, how could I control this power I hadn't known I had?

Though it did feel familiar, tickling my memory strangely as the storm seemed to grow once more, the room now almost pitch-black as the light was sucked out of the air.

Hands touched my neck and the taste of the memory grew stronger, the scent of water and dirt and blood permeating it like a bittersweet coating.

I'm sorry, love. They were the last words I heard before the world ended with a sharp crack.

CHAPTER TWENTY-ONE

HUNGER WAS ALL I KNEW WHEN I AWOKE. I WAS IN bed and the sheets covering me smelled of Hayes, relaxing me as well as heightening my need to feed.

I sat up and the sheets fell to my waist. At some point someone had changed me out of my clothes and into one of the skimpy nightdresses I'd found in my room—only this one was unfamiliar. Was Hayes the one slipping them into my room while I was gone? Did he have a collection of them in his room just for me?

The air was a cool rush over my skin and I stiffened when I felt eyes on me.

Hayes stepped forward, still half-shrouded in shadow as he watched me.

"What happened?" My voice was a dry rasp that made me wince but Hayes didn't move closer.

"You happened, love." His tone was fond but his words sounded strained. "I'm sorry."

"For what?" I said, rubbing my neck and then slowly lowering my hand as some of what had happened started to come back to me. Anger was a slow burn inside me as he took another step closer. "What did you do?"

His face was partially illuminated by a stripe of light from his window as he watched me, no remorse on his face. "If I hadn't done it, you would have killed yourself with the amount of power you were wielding."

I narrowed my eyes. "What. Did. You. Do."

"What I had to," he said, voice cold, and I nearly growled.

"Say it."

"I snapped your neck."

Bastard.

He moved before I could, appearing by the end of the bed and pinning me down as he leaned over. "I wasn't going to watch it consume you again, Leonora. I will always protect you," he murmured, adding as an afterthought, "even from yourself."

"Again?" I shoved him off of me, wanting answers before I could allow my hunger to win out and I became distracted. "The lake."

He nodded. "You were out of control, running high on blood and confused by the block in your mind—your rage drew your power to the surface and I thought it would be better for you to discover it on your own. Clearly I was wrong." He looked away, mouth a tight line on his face. "You thought I'd hurt the girl you'd killed."

Now he was saying it, I could picture it all perfectly. The way the sky had darkened as a storm unexpectedly rolled in, the grass greying beneath my feet as I pulled life from it to funnel my magick. Some of my anger abated, but only slightly.

"So you snapped my damn neck? *Again?*"

"Better a temporary death than a permanent one," he snapped and I hissed. "Your body was literally steaming from the power you contained. You may be immortal, but even an undead vampire wouldn't survive spontaneous combustion."

I'd thought Hayes was keeping his distance because he feared my anger, but now I could see him clearly and I realised he had kept his distance because of *his* anger.

"Damn right I'm angry," he said, face suddenly looming above mine as he clasped my jaw in his fingers. "I could feel you drowning in your own fucking magick, you were about two seconds away from burning from the inside out. I was two seconds away from *losing you*."

God, he cared. He really did care, even if it killed him.

The growl that left him was wild, a sound of pent-up anger, sorrow. His mouth found mine and I didn't try to resist the pull, my hands fisting roughly in his hair as he climbed onto the bed, straddling my body and gasping when I bit his lip and licked away the blood.

"Don't ever shut me out like that again," he said, the words a desperate plea that somehow sounded both reprimanding and tender.

"I didn't mean to," I said honestly and he didn't reply, only kissed me harder.

I didn't know if it was the bond or just something about *him* that made it difficult to do anything but give in when we kissed, but it was like my body was his for the taking.

Our kisses were rough, sloppy almost, his teeth biting into my mouth and trailing down over my chin and throat until he sank his teeth in and I gasped, arching up into him.

He didn't drink for long. Instead he smoothed one hand down my side and over my waist to curl around my hip as he pushed my legs open, settling between them in one fluid movement that had me aching. His mouth found my breasts, tugging the nightdress down roughly so I was exposed to the air as he bit down. It was like liquid fire had been poured into my veins as he drank, all my nerve endings coming alive as the pleasure mounted at the tip of my breast. Hayes' hands pushed higher, sliding under the tiny hem of the dress, closing on my arse and dragging me closer so he could press the hardest part of him against my softness.

I laughed breathlessly when he sat up with a curse and ripped the silk and lace straight down the middle. He looked at me like he was starving and pressed kisses to my stomach, licking and nipping at the skin as he made his way between my thighs. I tilted my hips up for him, and his answering smirk was pure smug satisfaction as he bit my inner thigh at the same time that one finger pushed into my pussy. He curled the digit and I ground down helplessly as he pulled from me in deep drags that only heightened the pleasure from his finger moving inside me.

I shivered at the remnants of red lingering on his lips when he looked up from between my thighs and licked the bite mark before he withdrew completely, sitting back and pulling off his shirt. His broad shoulders filled the space between my parted thighs as he sank back down and closed his mouth on my clit, the flat of his tongue drawing aching, torturous circles as he pressed his mouth in firmly.

My hands fisted in his crisp sheets and when I pulsed in time with the motion of his tongue he stopped, ignoring my whimpered protest as he flipped me over and the sound of his jeans hitting the ground followed shortly after.

Warmth hit me as his thighs weighed down the backs of mine, his hands smoothing their way up and down my spine as he kissed my neck, leaning down to bite my shoulder until I writhed underneath him.

He sat back up and his palms on my arse made me squirm as he parted the cheeks as he squeezed. A sharp sting made me yelp and I tried to peer back, grunting when his hand pushed my head back down into the bed. "Did you just bite my arse?"

He did it again, and I would have found it funny except I knew it was his vampiric side taking over, telling him to claim me in the best way a vampire knew how—through blood and sex. I must have truly been close to death for his instincts to react like this.

"Are you ready for me, Leonora?" His voice was rough, husky, and when he nudged at my entrance I pushed back eagerly. He spread my cheeks again and paused, making me pant with need before he finally thrust into me in one long motion. I clamped down around him eagerly and he growled when I tried to rise up to meet him.

His hand came down on the back of my neck, holding me flat and creating more friction between us as he fucked me punishingly.

I moaned his name and his voice was low when he spoke to me. "That's right, Leonora. Can you feel how easily I own this pussy? Do you know how fucking wet you are for me?"

He slowed his pace and the wet slide of his dick pushing inside me echoed in his room as he teased me. "On your knees," he hissed and I obeyed, too eager for the pleasure I knew he could wring from me to bristle at the command. His hand in the centre of my back ensured my chest remained flush with the bed as my arse hovered in the air like a corrupted prayer position.

I expected him to fill me again but when his fingers

pushed in instead I whined and they were quickly replaced by his dick. Heat pushed into me and I knew I was getting close to the edge when suddenly two fingers, slick from my pussy, pushed into my arse. The double sensation pushed me over the edge and I shook in front of him as he continued to fuck me, his thrusts growing rougher until he called my name.

I stayed still, breathing hard when he rolled off of me. I was sore, but in a good way, Hayes' bite marks already healing over.

"Feel better?" I remarked and he snorted as he made his way into the en suite connected to his room and turned the shower on.

"You coming?" He called to me a second later and I smiled as I stood up and followed him inside.

"WHAT IS HE DOING HERE?"

"I called him," Hayes said, closing the door to his room sharply after checking the corridor. "And he's not supposed to be here without Elowen's permission so keep your voice down."

I scowled, not fully trusting the mage after the last time we'd tried to trigger a memory of mine—though, I supposed he *had* said it would hurt. "Why did you call him? I don't have to drink more of that purple shit do I?"

Cal snorted and shook his head as he sat down in the chair tucked under the small desk Hayes had under his window. "Absolutely not. I think that's what got you into this mess."

I folded my arms across my chest, grateful for the long

shirt Hayes had provided me with after our long shower—I wouldn't have wanted to see the mage in the skimpy night dress even if it wasn't now shredded. "What mess would that be?"

"Oh, I don't know," Hayes said, matching my tone as he stood next to the mage, "maybe you generating more power than the sun?"

"There's no need to exaggerate." Fucking drama queen.

Hayes stared me down as Cal looked back and forth between us. "West was in a coma from just a quarter of what you were putting out, Leonora. You put an *undead vampire* into a *coma* that took him three hours to come out of." He paused and glanced at the mage before continuing, "And I don't think that was the full extent of it either—if you were trained, you might be able to wield more."

"Bet you're glad we're bonded now," I said faintly and the mage's eyes widened, like he hadn't put the dots together yet. "So why the mage?"

"Because none of the vampires here will be able to teach you the control necessary for the level of power you have."

I raised an eyebrow. "Seriously? So you're, what, going to train me?"

Cal nodded and I frowned.

"We think that maybe the potion opened your true power when it eased the barriers in your mind, but blocks are often there for a reason." Cal shot me a look as if to say *I told you so.* "You weren't ready to wield as much as you did."

I sighed, rubbing my temples. "Why is this happening to me?" I muttered and something flickered across the mage's face too quickly for me to parse out.

"It's not safe for you to wield around others," he said eventually and I bit my lip but didn't argue.

"Was anybody else hurt?" I asked Hayes and he shrugged.

"I was more interested in making sure you were alive."

"What about Rowan?" I still wasn't sure what their history was like, how serious they'd been, but surely Hayes would have at least checked our friend wasn't dead or hurt?

A small pinch marred his face and a flicker of guilt passed through the bond. He hadn't thought about it, and that bothered him. Our bond was taking over, but it was hard to be worried when it felt so good—and not just the sex or blood. The bond was more content when we were close, so of course it would affect things. Other priorities.

As if my words had conjured him, Rowan burst into the room a moment later. His eyes widened in relief when he saw me standing and recovered.

"Thank fuck," he said and the word sounded filthier coming out of his mouth for some reason—sexier. I hadn't even had time to reply before he was striding towards me and taking my cheeks in his hands, lifting my face to his as his mouth crashed down on mine.

Surprisingly, the bond didn't seem to mind. And I wasn't sure I minded either. His lips were harder than I'd expected, and his grip on me was firm. Always the quiet ones, I mused as he pulled away and I saw Novalie in the doorway too, looking bemused.

For the first time, Rowan seemed to notice Cal and his hands fell from my face like he'd been burned. "What is *he* doing here?"

"Helping," Hayes said, his face like thunder.

"Right," Rowan said, shaking his head as he stormed back towards the door. "Glad you're okay," he muttered and Novalie and I shared a look as they left that made me hide a laugh behind a cough.

Tension fell heavy in the air and Cal looked between Hayes and me before clearing his throat. "I'll just—"

"Get out," Hayes and I said at the same time, our eyes not leaving each other as Cal left the room too. "What was that?" he demanded and I raised my eyebrows.

"I think, correct me if I'm wrong, it was a kiss?"

Hayes scowled and his face looked more severe than usual with his hair slicked back after the shower. "Are you with him?"

"I'm standing here. With you."

He didn't know what to make of that and neither did I, if I was being honest.

I made my way back to the bed and patted the spot next to me. "Fine. Let's have it out. You and Rowan, was it serious?"

He shook his head as he sat down beside me. "No. It was casual, but we've always been on good terms."

I nodded. "That's the first time he's kissed me. Though we did come close a little while ago."

It didn't look like that thought sat well with Hayes.

"So, what. Are you jealous?" I had no idea if he wanted me, or if he was just satiating demands from the bond. Or maybe it was only about the blood.

"No," he said, answering my thoughts aloud, "it's more than the blood." He turned to me and his blue eyes were serious, darkening the longer he looked at me. "You've crawled under my skin and I don't think I could get you out with the sharpest knife in the world."

"I like you too," I said, rolling my eyes but he shook his head.

"I *do* like you, love. You drive me wild and I'm not sure at what point I went from wanting to kill you to shut you up and instead wanting to fuck you." I knew the feeling. Hayes smirked, clearly having heard. "Eternity is a long time, and vampires like to have fun. I'm not saying you can't pursue something with Rowan," he said with a frown, "but there's a difference between fun and love."

"And you love me?"

He shrugged. "I could."

"If you don't mind just sex, then why do you keep frowning every time we talk about Rowan?"

"There's something... I don't know. Off, with him lately."

Well, Hayes would know better than me, I didn't exactly have a reference point to compare. "We'll figure it out as we go then?"

Hayes nodded. "Together."

I nodded and we clasped hands, the deal struck.

"Do I really have to train with Cal?" I pouted as we fell back against the bed and Hayes laughed.

"You should give him a chance. I've known him since I was young, he's a good guy."

My smile faded. "Yeah, I don't know. I guess it's like you and Rowan, there's just something about him that doesn't feel right to me."

"Do you want me to come to training with you?"

I considered his offer, surprised. "It's going to take a while to get used to you being nice to me."

"I'll keep you on your toes," he promised. "SO, training?"

"When Cal says it's safe, then yes, please."

"Do you think this is the longest we've ever gone alone together without fighting or fucking?"

I snorted. "There's still time."

CHAPTER TWENTY-TWO

"I KNOW THIS WILL BE HARD FOR A VAMPIRE," CAL said with a sneer, "but in order to control your magick, you must control your emotions. For a new undead, this will be harder than it would for someone with experience."

"So you're telling me it's pointless?" We stood in the turret I'd found on my second day at Ashvale—it was large enough that we could move around if we needed to, and it was out of the way enough that we likely wouldn't bump into anyone else. I was getting better at focusing my senses even while I was distracted, so it was possible I'd actually hear someone coming up the stairs towards us if it happened.

"I'm telling you it's going to be hard and I'm telling you in advance because I don't want to listen to you whine."

I sniffed. "I don't whine."

Cal raised an eyebrow but didn't reply, instead he lifted his arms out to his side and clapped them together, conjuring a ball of blue fire that made me eye him appreciatively. Maybe he was useful after all. He whipped his hand like he held a lasso and I swore as the fire whipped out towards me. I darted to one side just in time and the mage smirked.

"Arsehole."

"Now, now, don't be jealous," he taunted and I scowled harder.

"What even is my power anyway?"

Cal let the fire dissipate and approached me. "Each time you've wielded it, you've conjured a storm. So it seems like it's based in the elements, aside from your resistance to compulsion."

"Are there any sire lines that specialise in that?"

He stilled, his eyes staying on mine when he answered. "Not as far as I can remember."

"Okay," I said slowly, weirded out by his hyper-focused response. "So what am I doing first? Rain? Lightning?"

"You," Cal said with a large amount of satisfaction that immediately had me on edge, "are going to stay calm."

That was all the warning he gave me before I was pelted with torrential rain. I couldn't hear anything over the banging of raindrops on the floorboards and my hair was quickly plastered to my head.

"What the fuck are you doing?" I roared and through the water streaming in my eyes I could see Cal laughing.

The rain turned to ice, small shards that sliced wounds in my skin that healed over just as fast, leaving smudges of dried blood on my exposed arms. I gritted my teeth and tried to ignore the sting. Stay calm. *Bastard.* He just wanted to score some free hits.

The ice eased and then stopped, leaving me glaring through my dripping hair at the mage, whose smile dimmed, an almost haunted expression taking root on his face.

"Good," he said gruffly and my anger faded, replaced by curiosity. "Again."

"Wait—" My frustrated shout was lost in the wind storm Cal conjured next. It whipped around me, lifting me off of my feet and I fought against it, not at all convinced that the mage wouldn't throw me off of the tower if he had the chance.

"Enough!" Power burst from me in an uncontrolled wave of chaos and I paused, stupefied as it flew at Cal. He dug his feet in and crouched slightly, raising his hands and wrapping my power in a bubble of his own design, forcing it smaller until it winked out of existence with a clap like thunder.

Cal panted and I stayed perfectly still. "It's enough when I say it is. You might be powerful, little vamp, but you've got nothing on me."

I looked him up and down, warily. It was true that he'd handled that wave just fine, but he looked to be in his late thirties. Hardly an ancient wizard.

He smirked like he could see what I was thinking. "I'm older than I look. " At my doubt he turned away and walked so that there was more space between us. "Give it your best shot."

I didn't really know how to trigger my magick, so instead, I went for the throat. I choked, held in place by an invisible hand about a metre away from Cal.

"I'm one-hundred-and-twenty-seven. I can do things with magick you couldn't even dream about. If you pay attention, maybe you'll learn how to master some of them too."

I backed away as soon as the magickal grip let up. "Fine."

He nodded, satisfied now we'd had our pissing contest. "Again."

By the time I walked back down from the turret, I actually ached from being abused by elemental magick. I knew I would heal relatively quickly—faster if I drank some blood, but it still wasn't pleasant having my arse handed to me over and over while Cal barked at me to stay calm.

He'd declared we were done after an hour and a half and had simply disappeared, which was admittedly pretty cool.

I could only blame my inattentiveness on my temporary exhaustion, my mind elsewhere, as I walked down the second set of stairs, emerged on the top floor of the castle, and promptly tripped.

"What the fuck—" I looked down and felt fear clog my throat. How had this happened to me twice? A pair of legs stuck out from the corner next to the stairs, and the body hadn't stirred when I fell which told me at least one thing.

I stepped closer anyway, pressing two fingers to the guy's neck and backing away quickly when I felt no pulse. I turned away, unsure who to call or how to contact anyone up here on the top floor. I called to Hayes and felt his alarm when he felt my worry.

I'm coming.

I sagged with relief and turned back to the body before freezing up. A set of bloody footprints led away from the vampire on the floor and over to the window. Whoever had done this had jumped down into the grass outside, a small dent marking their landing. I moved away from the window when I heard Hayes coming up the stairs and then gasped as I turned, my hand instinctively flying up to cover my mouth. I wasn't generally a squeamish person, but I hadn't expected to see a half-eaten heart on the floor when I'd looked back at the body from this angle.

Hayes was there in a flash, running his hands over me as if to check for injuries before he followed the line of my eyes and swore.

Whoever had killed this living vampire had to have been angry or insane to have ripped out their heart and fed directly from it.

"Can he regenerate it?" I whispered and Hayes lifted one shoulder and dropped it again.

"Some can, some can't. I think it depends on the strength of the vampire. The transition can repair a lot of damage but if the head or heart isn't intact then it makes things a lot less likely."

"So he's probably true dead, then?"

"Likely," another voice cut in and I nearly jumped. Elowen. She'd moved so quietly I hadn't heard her approach.

She looked down at the victim dispassionately, heaving a sigh before waving us off. "One of the first years probably lost control of their hunger. I'll take care of this."

I tried to hide my surprise and glanced at Hayes to see him doing the same. "You think it's just coincidence that another body has been found just days after Emerson?"

Elowen shrugged one elegant shoulder, sweeping her dark hair away from her face with her fingers as she stared us down. "I don't see what one has to do with the other."

"Well two is a coincidence, three is a pattern," I pointed out and she laughed coldly.

"Or you go to a school filled with hungry vampires who are still learning to find their control. That," she said sharply as I opened my mouth to reply, "is quite enough MIss

Romilly. I won't have you causing unnecessary panic. Now why don't you run along and dry yourself off?"

I'd barely noticed that I was still wet after training with Cal, but I had no choice but to nod and let Hayes walk with me down the stairs as Elowen stared at us.

When I figured we were far enough out of earshot, I turned to him. "This is your second year—is this really as common as she's making it out to be?"

He shook his head. "How to feed is one of the first training sessions you have here— sure, a few people died or were accidentally turned but not like this, not one after another."

That was what I'd thought. Which meant my instincts had been right about Elowen from the start. "She's hiding something," I murmured and could tell that the thought troubled Hayes just as much as it did me.

~

"YOU KNOW, YOU REALLY DON'T HAVE TO STAY with me every night." I watched, amused, as Hayes fluffed the side of the bed that had now been dubbed as 'his'. He'd decided that he would be staying with me from now on until whoever or whatever was causing the deaths of all these vampires was put to rest.

He patted the bed next to him. "Shut up and get in bed. I'm not going anywhere."

I laughed but did as he said, turning out the light on my bedside. My smile faded as I thought about what he *wasn't* saying. "You think it's going to get worse, don't you?"

He hesitated, but I didn't really need him to say

anything. I could feel his constant worry through the bond like it was my own.

"I think that whatever this is, isn't over."

There had been two more bodies found that week—one in the woods completely drained and the other was only discovered because the living vampire awoke as an undead and nearly murdered the living vampire next door.

"Plus, with the debut coming up so soon, I think all the undead vampires around won't help with controlling bloodlust."

My thoughts churned as I lay there quietly, thinking about Emerson and Novalie and Rowan—we'd told them about our suspicions and had received varied responses back: Fear (Emerson), Doubt (Rowan), and Intrigue (Novalie).

I cleared my throat and voiced one of the things that had been bothering me for the last few days. "It doesn't make sense. It has to be more than one vampire because I killed Colin," I rolled my eyes at the name. "And the bloody footprints in the hall were very different to the ones in Carys' room." At the question I could feel from his side of the bond I added, "I snuck in before Elowen could scrub all the evidence away."

"So something is happening to increase the bloodlust of several vampires—but not all of us. What could be affecting them?"

"The food?" I suggested and Hayes shook his head, hair rustling against the pillow.

"No, otherwise one of us would have experienced it at some point too."

"Maybe it's a bloodline thing?" I was doubtful though, it seemed unlikely that some kind of mental instability or disease wouldn't have been found before now if it ran in the sire line.

"I doubt it," Hayes said, echoing my thoughts.

"So it must be something they're voluntarily doing then. Or something they don't realise is being done to them," I mused. "We're in an academy full of nineteen-to-twenty-year-olds. Maybe we're overlooking the obvious."

"Drugs?" Hayes sounded surprised and I chuckled.

"I knew you weren't just a pretty face." I rolled to face him, tracing the outline of his silhouette with my eyes in the dark. "Humans get bad batches of drugs all the time. Do you think it's possible?"

"Maybe, I'll have to ask Cal."

I scowled at the reminder of the mage. My control was improving. Slightly. But his methods still left much to be desired. "So theoretically, as long as we don't take anything we shouldn't then we should be alright."

"Unless whoever's dealing is actually dosing," Hayes said, a darkness in his voice that made me scoot closer, draping one leg over his.

"Do you think I made a mistake with Emerson?" I asked, changing the subject to avoid whatever darkness lurked in Hayes' memories. "Turned vampires are rare, right?"

"I don't think it will ever be a mistake to try and help someone the way you did." I smiled a little at his words, pleased. "Besides, you technically made history."

"I did?"

"In several ways," he said, and it sounded like pride in his voice. "You might be the youngest person to ever turn another through bite or blood, but you've also technically started a new sire line."

I blinked, floored. "Wow."

"Yeah. So whatever does or doesn't happen at the debut ball... Emerson will always have a home with you, and vice versa."

"And you," I interjected without thinking. "Um, I mean, if you want."

He was quiet for a moment and I worried I'd upset him somehow. "I'd like that."

I blew out a quiet breath—we were already tied together intrinsically, but it was different to *choose* to tie ourselves to each other. "How did you meet Cal, by the way? You said you knew him when you were young."

I wasn't sure if it was an effort to share more that made him finally answer, or if it just felt safe to be vulnerable in the safety of darkness, but I could feel the pain in Hayes when he answered. "He's indebted to my family, so I've known him for as long as I've lived—the only time we've been apart was when I was living my mortal life."

"He's like family, then."

Hayes shrugged. "He didn't start out that way—but now he's all I have left.""

I wanted to ask more, a million questions burning inside of me, but I could also feel exactly how this was hurting him, so I just kissed him on the cheek and let my eyes slide closed.

"I'll try to be nicer to him then."

Hayes' quiet chuckle followed me into sleep.

Chapter Twenty-Three

"Good," Cal called and I let my hands fall warily. He liked to pretend we were done training and then spring a surprise attack on me to test me. Or so he claimed. I was pretty sure he just liked any opportunity to try and knock me on my arse.

When no other attack came, I relaxed. Cal's hand whipped out and I smirked, having anticipated that he would wait until I let my guard down to try something. I brought my hands up in front of me in a cross formation and his cheap shot bounced harmlessly off of the shield of storm I'd conjured, miniature dark clouds swirling angrily in a breeze that was self-contained and lightning bolts flashing harmlessly within the grey. I was nowhere near perfect, but I had a small amount of control now. I just wanted to move beyond shielding to something actually cool.

He grunted and I knew he was pleased. We'd trained every day for the last week and a half and so maybe it was foolish for me to want to learn something new—like trying to run before you could walk. I opened my mouth to ask anyway and Cal rolled his eyes, having anticipated this as I usually asked him at least once per session if we could move on to offensive training.

"Just one thing," I needled, approaching him as he stood looking faintly amused. "Show me how to throw a lightning bolt or something."

He laughed and that wasn't the response I'd been hoping for. "You're not ready for that yet. But fine, you want to learn something? Let's see how far your connection to the elemental goes." There was a glint in his eyes that told me he thought he already knew the answer.

That was fine, he was finally going to teach me something beyond how to shield and I didn't care what it was.

He stepped closer to me and I tried not to show my surprise. Most mages tolerated but disliked vampires, though I supposed he was more comfortable than most thanks to his history with Hayes.

He took my hands in his and it felt strange, there was a gentleness in his denim gaze that I'd never seen before. "Close your eyes."

It was a testament to how far we'd come that I obeyed. I trusted him enough that Hayes didn't come to all of our sessions any more, and he trusted me enough to know that I was mostly kidding when I threatened to bite him.

Cal held his hands outside of mine on either side with a large gap in between my palms.

"I want you to focus," he murmured and I resisted the urge to snark at him. "Think of warmth, lazy heat, fire, light. I want you to bring it forth in your mind until you can almost taste it."

I obeyed, thinking about campfires and lazy beach days,

the heat of the sand scalding my feet and making my head feel fuzzy.

"Open your eyes," Cal said softly.

Light filled the turret, spilling out of the window like a beacon. I flinched back a little. I had noticed that the more time I'd spent using my magick, the more sensitive to the sun I was becoming.

Cal dropped his hands and the ball of light faded. "You can control the power of the light by funnelling more or less magick into it, similar to how you can adjust the strength or size of your shield." I nodded and he looked uncharacteristically worried. "I don't know what's happening around here, Leonora, but you need to be careful. There's no greater weakness for the undead vampire than sunlight—think of this trick as an ace in the hole, one that will buy you time to run."

I knew what he wasn't saying—that if I found myself in that situation, running would be my best chance for survival. Raw power didn't mean anything if I couldn't control it.

"Did Hayes ask you about the drugs yet?" I walked over to the window to peer outside at the light fog rolling in through the trees. It was going to rain, and somehow the scent of it in the air soothed me.

"Yes. I spoke to him this morning."

"And? Do you think it's possible?"

Cal joined me at the window, hesitating before speaking. "Anything is possible when it comes to magick. But I haven't heard of anything like this before. I've put out some feelers in the community to see if there has been any chatter."

I nodded absently. "Why would someone want to make living vampires lose control?" Cal shrugged, turning his back to the outside and leaning against the wall next to me. "Why does anyone do anything? Money? Power? Hate?"

I watched him assessing before turning back to the window. We would need to leave soon—someone had almost definitely seen the light spilling out of here and would come poking around.

I pushed away from the wall and paused when Cal spoke again. "You're good for him, you know. Hayes," he added, like he could have been referring to anyone else.

"How so?"

"I know neither of you asked for this bond, but he can't push you away now even if he wanted to—and he does have a tendency to do that."

"I don't think either of us expected to find anything like what the bond has given us."

"But?"

I smiled and turned back towards the stairs. "But sometimes the universe knows what you need better than you do ." I chanced a glance back and was unsurprised to find the room empty—I was going to badger him into teaching me that trick soon.

I made my way downstairs, my gaze instinctively finding the spot where the body had lain not so long ago. Nothing marred the floor, not a speck of blood remained.

I turned away and continued making my way through the corridors and down the stairs until I bumped into Emerson.

I used a burst of speed to reach her side and grinned when she jumped. She'd settled in well and was becoming fast friends with Novalie, which I appreciated. I couldn't be with her all the time and it was good to know someone else was watching out for her.

"Training?" she asked and I nodded.

"Where are you off to?"

She grimaced, somehow managing to make the expression look attractive. "Extra feeding lessons for those of us Elowen feels may be more prone to slipping." Emerson rolled her eyes and fluffed her hair. "I mean, no offence but I have better self-control than you and I don't see you attending remedial feeding."

I snorted. "Thanks. Your hair looks nice, by the way."

"Novalie helped me take out some of the braids," she said, smiling slightly and I couldn't help but watch her in admiration. She'd adjusted surprisingly well to being a vampire—better than I had, that was for sure. I wondered if it was because she'd had closure about her murder, where I still had yet to find mine.

"I'm okay," she said knowingly and pressed a quick kiss to my cheek before hurrying off to her class. "Be good!"

I smiled. It was like I'd told Cal, sometimes you didn't know what you needed until it walked into your life. I felt that way about Emerson too. She was strong in ways I wasn't sure I would ever be and, surprisingly, she felt more alive than some of the living vampires did.

"Feeling melancholy?" a familiar voice murmured in my ear as arms slipped around my waist.

"Maybe a little." I smiled as I faced Hayes. "Checking up on me?"

"Just making sure you hadn't killed anyone yet today," he teased.

"It's still early." I smirked and loved that his eyes darkened with desire instead of fear or disgust. I didn't make a habit of killing people, but I also didn't have as many qualms about violence now—maybe that was Hayes' influence bleeding into me from the bond, or maybe I was just changing. It didn't scare me as much anymore, not with all the death in the castle recently. Sometimes you had to bite or be bitten.

"Hungry?" His voice had a deeper note to it that made my fangs ache in anticipation.

"When it comes to you? Always."

CHAPTER TWENTY-FOUR

EMERSON KNOCKED ON MY DOOR LATER THAT evening and Hayes raised an eyebrow at me, tugging the sheets up slightly to hide his lack of clothes.

I opened the door and concern immediately hit me. She looked rattled, her eyes darting to the left and right of the corridor before she hurried into my room and shut the door.

"Can you put something in place so we won't be overheard? Like with your magick?" she said before I could say anything.

Hayes nodded, his dark brows furrowing as he watched us. A breeze blew past me and I knew Hayes had locked a shield of air around us as I watched, impressed. I hadn't even known that was something he could do.

"What's wrong?" I asked immediately and Emerson sat down heavily on the end of my bed, her dark eyes wide and her breaths uneven. She was panicking. "Hold your breath," I advised, and she blew out slowly before doing as I suggested.

"I didn't know what it was, Leonora. I promise. They

just said it would make us feel good—like, high. But now I feel..."

"Hungry," I whispered, chills running through me. "Who gave it to you?" I said urgently, as Hayes stood and tugged on some joggers, wariness settling into his face as he watched Emerson. I shot him a look, she wasn't going to hurt us.

"One of the living vampires," she muttered, twisting her fingers in her lap. "I was sitting with Novalie in the food hall—"

Shit. She had said *us*. "Did she take it too?"

Emerson nodded and I swore again. Emerson was right, she did have great self control, hopefully it wouldn't hurt her too badly or maybe it would affect her differently as a turned vampire, but Novalie... Well, she was impulsive at the best of times.

"Leonora," Emerson said quietly and I paused, having moved to my door without thinking too much about it. Someone needed to stop Novalie before she did something she'd regret. "Leah, I think they were deliberately targeting people from the remedial feeding class and Novalie just got caught in the crossfire."

It was somewhere to start, other than hunting down the dealer the girls had seen. I nodded to her and raised a hand when Hayes moved to follow me.

"No, you stay here with Emerson. If this does suddenly hit her hard we'll need someone here. Plus, you've been enough of a temptation to Novalie in the past that I don't want to push her."

Hayes nodded reluctantly and I pulled open my door as he dissolved the air shield, a small breeze stroking across my cheek as he watched me go. *Be safe.*

I ran to Novalie's room first and found it empty, so then I tried the library—also empty. I let out a slow breath. I was going to need to focus if I wanted to find her.

I closed my eyes and tried to let the world fall away as I listened for her. I dismissed the snatches of conversation I heard through the walls, trying to narrow in on her voice.

Nothing.

Fuck. Where could she be?

I wracked my brains and decided to check the hall used to serve food. It was unlikely she'd be there, but I wasn't sure what else to try.

I reached the doors in mere seconds and scanned the tables for her. Most were empty, but... Wasn't that the girl Novalie fancied? Sarah? Sienna?

Siera, I finally recalled as I strode to her table and pushed my hair behind my ear as I stopped before her, a human gesture meant to set her at ease. It worked, sort of.

"Have you seen Novalie?"

Her eyes were sharp as they assessed me before deciding I wasn't asking because I wanted to hurt her. "Not since this afternoon."

I blew out a breath but nodded my thanks and walked back out the way I'd come, but heading towards the back door that led outside instead of upstairs. I needed air.

What if she'd gone to the nearest town? I bit my lip as the cool air rushed over me, and I relaxed. Normally, Novalie wouldn't do that—but who knew what this drug might make her want to do?

The wind shifted direction and I turned to go back inside when a rich scent carried to me on the breeze.

Blood.

It had an undercurrent of citrus, like Novalie's shampoo

and I stood there for a second, unsure what I'd find in the woods if I went looking. We may have had a rocky start, but I liked Novalie. I didn't want to find her dead—and it was definitely her blood I smelled and not anyone else's.

I walked reluctantly into the trees, the moon providing a sliver of light but mostly I had to rely on my senses to make it through without falling and accidentally staking myself on a branch.

The smell of blood grew heavier and I froze when I heard Novalie's cry of pain—did we have this all wrong? Was someone hurting her?

I didn't waste any more time, just dodged the trees as I ran to her. Fear was an acrid taste in my mouth as I found her inches away from the clearing I'd stumbled across before. Blood slicked her arms and she was dangerously pale, pinned to the floor of the forest by two thick branches through her palms and a blade through her shoulder.

I dropped to my knees and reached for one of the branches as she snarled at me.

"No! Leave it in."

I hesitated, confused as I took in the wildness of her eyes and the sheen of sweat on her forehead. "Who the fuck did this? Let me take you back to the castle." I frowned as I got a better look at the blade. It was her own.

"Don't take me back there," she panted. "I can't control it—"

"Emerson told us what happened," I cut in and she growled as I got too close, her teeth snapping dangerously close to my arm. "Did you do this to yourself?" I asked quietly and she sobbed.

"It fucking hurts, Nora. It's hunger like I've never felt it, like it'll tear me up and consume me if I don't drink."

I sat down next to her at a safe distance, amused by the plethora of nicknames for me that had emerged today. I didn't mind though, not really. It felt like... belonging.

"It's okay," I soothed. "It'll pass. I'll stay here with you the whole time."

"Thank you," she whispered and I let a small tendril of magick slip out of me—water to clean away her blood and a small gust of wind to blow away the scent of it, no doubt the smell wasn't helping her hunger any.

"Why did you take it?" Maybe if we knew what the appeal was, we could better shut this shit down. "Do you remember who gave you the drugs?" I wanted to distract her, but it was also an important question that couldn't wait.

"I-I wanted to be strong. Like you. They said it would make us feel strong, like an undead, but we could still have the sun."

Well, fuck. I could kind of understand the temptation now—but what those bastards weren't telling their customers was that alongside the increased strength clearly came an increased hunger. Magick always had a cost.

"Who gave it to you?" I winced as her arms continued slowly seeping blood, the smell of it slightly strange like the drugs had altered it in some way.

"One of Colin's friends. Dean or something?" she said, voice hoarse from screaming as she'd nailed herself to the ground.

I had no idea what anyone's name was but I nodded anyway. It made sense that Colin's friend group were at the centre of this mess. But the real question was where were they getting the drugs from? I couldn't imagine they were intelligent enough to cook up something like that by themselves.

"Is Emerson okay?" Novalie asked after a second and I nodded.

"Yeah, I don't know if it's just her excellent control or if it's because she was turned and not born, but it doesn't seem to be hitting her as hard. I left her with Hayes."

A low snarl left Novalie at his name and I tried not to retaliate, pushing my instincts down sharply, knowing it was the drugs and not her that was in control.

"Sorry," she rasped and I smiled.

"Don't worry about it. What was it you took, anyway? Powder? Pill?"

"Powder." She squirmed against the forest floor, the leaves rustling beneath her as she fought against the hunger coursing through her. "Promise me I can rip off Dean's head."

"I promise." The words seemed to soothe her and I grinned.

I sat there with her for hours, shushing her when she whimpered, and it was only as the sky began to lighten that she slumped back against the ground, the feverish glaze clearing from her eyes

"I think it's over," she said weakly, and I immediately ripped the branches and blade from her, pulling her body into my lap as I pressed my wrist to her mouth. She had lost a lot of blood, and if she didn't feed immediately then this would all have been for nothing.

Novalie groaned as her teeth sank into my arm, and I stroked her hair back from her face. The colour returned to her cheeks after a few minutes, her wounds healing over with the aid of my blood.

"I'm going to rip him apart," Novalie said a few seconds later, placing a palm on a nearby tree as she swayed.

"Sleep first," I said with a snort. "Murder later."

CHAPTER TWENTY-FIVE

"REMIND ME WHAT WE'RE DOING AGAIN?" ROWAN asked as we sat at a table watching Dean and his loud group of friends laughing and shoving each other like extras in a teen movie a few tables over.

"You're going to buy drugs," I said simply and Emerson snickered.

"Why me?"

"Because Emerson and Novalie have already spoken to him and they all tend to run away when I get close." I smirked as I caught the eye of one of the vamps on Dean's table and flashed my fangs at him, snorting when he paled.

"See? That one nearly just wet himself."

"Fine." Rowan sighed. "Wait a couple minutes and then follow me."

Dean, or whatever his name was, stood up and walked out with Rowan a few minutes later and we all shared a look before hurrying after them. Probably conspicuous, but I couldn't bring myself to care. Let them know we were coming for them.

Are you up to mischief? Hayes' voice drifted to me and I felt a rush of warmth.

Maybe.

His laugh made me feel strangely gooey, but at Novalie's raised eyebrow I refocused on our mission.

Rowan had taken Dean around the side of the castle, partially hidden around a curve in the wall, but when he saw me coming his face whitened.

"Is this the guy?" I confirmed as I looked to Novalie and Emerson. They nodded, Novalie's eyes gleaming with her lust for revenge.

He tried to run and Rowan grabbed a fistful of his shirt and slammed him against the stone wall.

"Thank you," I said, pleased as I swapped Rowan's hand for my own. "We just have a few questions for you, Dean."

"Dane," he muttered and I raised an eyebrow.

"Close enough." I pursed my lips as I considered him. "Who gave you the drugs?"

His eyes flicked to each of us, as if looking for someone sympathetic and coming up empty.

"It would be better if you answered us," I said, leaning in close. My thrall skills were not that good yet, but I tried anyway. "Tell me what I want to know."

He swallowed, sweat breaking out across his skin as his head tossed back and forth. I didn't think he was particularly strong-minded, so this had to be something else.

"I don't think he can tell you," Rowan said and continued when I looked questioningly at him. "I think he's already been enthralled not to tell. By someone more powerful than you, I'm guessing."

"Well that *is* a shame. I guess you're of no use to us then."

Dane's eyes widened. "No. Please. I only did what I was told—"

"And look where it got you," I said pityingly, patting him down until I found two small baggies of powder on him.

"We should report this to Elowen." Rowan touched my arm and I wrinkled my nose, not liking the idea, primarily because I didn't trust Elowen as far as I could throw her— even if that was a significantly greater distance now I was a vampire. He continued staring at me expectantly and I shrugged.

"I'm not your mother. If you want to tell her then go ahead." I handed him one of the baggies as he held out his hand.

"Aren't you coming?"

"We'll be right behind you." I smiled and his eyes narrowed.

"Don't kill him," he said, mouth turning down as he watched me and I nodded sincerely.

"I won't." Which was true enough, I thought as Rowan disappeared inside. After all, I'd promised Dane to Novalie. "He's all yours."

Her wide smile even unnerved me a little as she stepped up to Dane. "I staked myself through both hands to stop myself from going on a killing spree, you piece of shit. I had to lie there, bleeding, for hours. Because of you."

"You chose to do the drugs!" he protested and Emerson shook her head, disgust lining her face.

"We never would have taken it if we'd known what it actually did," she said, moving to stand at Novalie's side. "You said it would make us feel good. That we would be stronger, faster. If you apologise, maybe we'll kill you quickly."

His face twisted into a sneer. "I'm not apologising for some bit-for-nothing, turned vamp."

Novalie struck him so hard I was surprised his neck didn't snap from the force of the blow. "Fucker," she spat and Emerson looked grim but satisfied, happy to let Novalie take the lead as she grabbed Dane's chin and forced it up. She stared into his eyes and I watched in vague interest as she enthralled him. "When I tell you, this is going to hurt worse than anything you've ever felt. Like you're being torn apart from the inside by a fire that wants to consume you."

I let out a low whistle but didn't stop her. It was the same way she'd described the drug's effect on her.

"An eye for an eye," Emerson murmured, coming to stand back next to me and I nodded.

Novalie struck, her fangs sinking deeply into his neck. The bite was messy and rivulets of blood slipped down Dane's throat. Novalie pulled back to look at him, spitting his blood out of her mouth like she didn't want a single part of him in her. Dane's eyes were wide, like shock was setting in and Novalie smiled. "Remember what I said?"

Still held in her thrall, Dane nodded.

"Good. Because this one's going to hurt."

She struck and Dane screamed.

～

"I CAN'T THANK YOU ALL ENOUGH FOR BRINGING this to my attention," Elowen said as she stood up from behind her desk to study each of us, and then moved to the front and perched against it in that classic 'we're equals' way that teachers often employed. "I will find out who is supplying this drug—but in the meantime, I don't want anybody leaving the sanctuary grounds. Who knows what people might bring in from outside?"

Noavlie gasped. "But what about the debut?" Elowen raised an eyebrow and Novalie explained, "We need to go shopping. I don't have a dress!"

"I feel that the lives of the students here at Ashvale are of a higher value than your need to go dress shopping," Elowen said and I wanted to laugh. I didn't know if it was some kind of magickal ability or what, but I just knew that every word out of her mouth was a lie.

She didn't care about the vampires, or their safety, which begged the question: why did she want to keep us trapped? More than that, a disregard for life and casual outlook on violence was one thing—but to actively *thank* us for dispatching Dane? It stank of bullshit.

Elowen's eyes met mine, a bottomless pool of brown, and I looked back at her just as shrewdly as she brushed a strand of dark, silky hair out of her face. "Given the circumstances, I'll let the condition of Dane slide, but let's not make a habit of murdering other students, hm?"

"Lots of paperwork involved?" I said with faux-sympathy and Elowen smiled, pulling her face taut.

"You may be excused." The door to her office flew open and we made our way to it before she stopped me. "Leonora, a word."

Novalie shot me a look of concern and I waved her off. Truth be told, I was curious to see what kind of bullshit would come out of Elowen's mouth next.

The door closed softly behind Rowan and I stayed standing even as she sat.

"I just wanted to apologise for not taking you seriously before—I truly felt that the deaths were commonplace. I see now that I was wrong."

I waited, expecting more, and smiling faintly when silence reigned.

"Is that all?" I asked, injecting as much polite cheer as I could into my voice.

"Yes. But Leonora," she said as I placed my hand on the door to leave, "be careful. Whoever is out there doing this likely won't be happy with your interference."

"I'll bear that in mind."

"See that you do."

I closed the door behind me and was unsurprised to find Hayes waiting around the corner, the warmth in the bond having already told me where he would be.

He opened his mouth and I shook my head, waiting until we were further away before I spoke. "I don't know what it is, but she's definitely hiding something. She *apologised* to me—since when do undead vampires do anything like that?"

Hayes frowned. "Maybe she was just being nice?"

I gave him a look that showed exactly how ridiculous I found that, and he nodded in agreement. "I can't explain it," I said carefully, keeping my voice hushed as we walked to Hayes' room. "But when she opens her mouth I just get this feeling, like a cold shiver, and I *know* she's lying."

"Does it happen with anyone else?" he asked, pushing his door shut and I shook my head.

"I don't think so."

"Hm."

"What?"

"Well, it just reminds me of Cal. He's mentioned a similar phenomena to me before."

"Phenomena," I echoed. "Good word."

Hayes rolled his eyes. "I'm being serious—what if we're missing something here? Your powers, your resistance to enthrallment, and now the ability to tell truth from lies? Those are all the qualities of a mage."

"What are you saying?" My stomach dipped and Hayes slid a small phone out of his pocket. I knew who he was dialling even before he spoke.

"I'm saying, I think one of your parents might have been a mage."

"Is that even possible?"

"Rare," Hayes murmured, "but not impossible." There was a click over the phone and Hayes said simply, "I need you," before hanging up.

The air seemed to shimmer or crackle and Cal stepped into the room like it was easy to appear from nothingness.

"What is it?" He looked between us, the concern evident on his face and making the fine lines there look more noticeable.

"Leonora can tell the difference between truth and lies," Hayes began and Cal looked like he'd been hit over the head. "Yeah, that's what I thought. What do you know that you haven't told us?"

"I know a lot of things," Cal said weakly and Hayes growled.

"Don't fuck with me. Speak."

"I'd hoped it wasn't true. I didn't think she would lie to me like that." A lead weight sank through my body, rooting me to the floor as Cal looked up and searched my face. "But I suppose I was just lying to myself—after all, you look so much like her."

If my heart worked, I had the feeling it would have been beating so quickly I might have thrown up.

"Like who?"

Cal sighed. "Your mother."

CHAPTER TWENTY-SIX

"Explain." I didn't recognise my voice and I definitely didn't recognise the man sitting in front of me. The one who might be my... "*Explain*," I repeated with more emphasis.

"What do you want me to say? I fell in love with a woman who I think was just using me to get close to... Well, it doesn't matter now. She told me she was pregnant, and for a while we were happy—but then she had an accident."

"She transitioned," I whispered and Cal nodded. "*You?*"

He nodded, watching me closely. "She changed after that. She told me she'd lost the baby and then she left. She had become... cold."

"You really didn't know?" Hayes said and Cal looked me straight in the eyes, the disbelief clear on his face.

"I had no idea you were alive, not until you turned up on my doorstep—and even then, I wasn't sure. You could have been anyone. It could have been coincidence."

"Who is she?" I sounded calm, which was a miracle, because inside I was a mess.

He shook his head. "She moved, just up and left. Changed her name, everything. I knew her as Isabella. I never learned of her sire line, some of the undead can be precious about the information."

I sat down heavily on the end of the bed. Was it possible for undead vampires to get migraines? Because it felt like I had the mother of them all brewing. "So what does that make me?"

Cal stood and approached me hesitantly, stopping when I stiffened. "Unique, as far as I know. It's not forbidden for a mage to be with a vampire, but it is frowned upon. Most of us dislike vampires too much to ever want to bed one."

"So I am a freak." I shook my head, standing up again, I needed to move. To run. "Half-mage. Half-vampire."

"You're the same person you've always been," Hayes protested and I laughed humorlessly.

"And who is that exactly? Because I sure don't remember."

"Leonora—"

"I need to get some air, okay? Don't follow me."

The door closed behind me and it felt strange, like the corridor should have looked different now that everything had shifted. It was just empty though, and it made me feel hollowed out inside. I instinctively turned to find the stairs and go outside, but stopped. I didn't think running from this was going to help. Forgetting about it, however, would absolutely help.

I turned instead in the direction of the library, hurrying along so I could hide between the stacks and find some text to bury myself in. Anything so I didn't have to contemplate what was coming next.

Cal was... I shook the thought away. Cal was Cal. My biology didn't change that.

The lights were low when I walked into the room, the smell of dust and paper comforting me in a way that made me wonder if I'd been a librarian or bookseller in my 'human' life.

I drew up short when I walked to the usual table and found Rowan there.

"Sorry, I'll just—"

"Wait, Leonora, you don't have to go. Not because of me."

We hadn't spoken about the kiss he'd given me after I'd nearly died from channelling too much magick. I guess I'd gotten good at avoiding the things I didn't want to deal with, I thought sourly. Though, admittedly, Rowan had shown no interest in wanting to kiss me again—probably on account of the murders I'd taken part in recently, or maybe it was because I was tied to his ex for eternity. A laugh bubbled out of me and I choked it down. Now wasn't the time for some kind of breakdown. I had the rest of my life to process my trauma, for now, I needed to get my shit together.

"Did something happen?" he said, taking a step closer when I didn't move and I shook my head, unsure what to say. I also didn't like how pro-Elowen he seemed to be. I didn't trust her and, by extension, I couldn't trust him. But I wanted to—god, did I want to.

"Just one of those days," I said and he looked disappointed but retreated back to the table, pushing a chair out for me with his foot when he sat down.

I accepted gratefully and it was quiet for a second as we watched each other. "Have you been avoiding me?" I finally asked and his answering smile was lopsided and embarrassed.

"Maybe a little. I shouldn't have kissed you."

I shrugged. "It's okay. It was a nice kiss, if a bit surprising."

"I've missed you," he said quietly, and I smiled.

"I think I was avoiding you too."

"Well, you're here now."

I pulled a book from his stack towards me. "What are we reading?" I swallowed when I read the title. "You're still looking into memory-recovery techniques?"

He shrugged, his cheeks flushing a light pink. "I wanted to help."

"Thank you." I opened my mouth and then closed it again. "Just... Thank you."

"Anytime," he murmured and I looked back down at the book with a smile.

"Do you think I could track down a vampire with just their first name using the genealogy books?"

Rowan frowned, biting the tip of a pen he was using to jot down notes. "Maybe, I guess it depends on how common the name is. Why?"

"No reason," I said quietly, not sure I was ready to go down that rabbit hole yet. Maybe some things were better off a mystery—after all, this was a mother that had stolen me away from my father and then essentially abandoned me in the human world. If she came for me after the debut, I honestly didn't know what I would do.

CHAPTER TWENTY-SEVEN

LAUGHTER ECHOED IN THE ALLEY AND WARMTH found me in a pair of brown eyes, long-lashed peering up from the pages of the book. The library twisted and morphed around me until I was back in the alley, laughter pouring out of my chest, the world oddly dizzy. Someone walked next to me, a vague outline, but I felt safe. Until I fell. My knee scraped the floor, my hands flew out to catch me and gravel dug into my skin, slicing me open. Then nothing but pain, the cold of the pavement sinking into my skin, my bones, warmth pooling at my throat and eyes different to those in the library—these were hungry, starved, even as horror filled them. Red bled into the sky as I looked up and I was drowning in it as—

I startled awake as hands clamped down on my shoulders.

"Wake up, love. You were dreaming."

I stilled, recognising Hayes' scent, his warmth tucked at my side as his fingers left my shoulders and ran through my hair.

"I knew him," I whispered and Hayes stilled.

"Knew who?"

"The man who killed me. Before it happened, I felt safe. I was laughing. But then I fell—I think the blood triggered him."

"You think the vampire who killed you was taking the drug," Hayes guessed and I nodded.

"I think... I think he apologised as I was bleeding out." A sharp stab of anger and fear that wasn't my own made me place one hand on his chest. "I'm okay. I'm here. Alive. Ish."

He chuckled and I relaxed back against him.

"I won't let anyone hurt you again," he said and I breathed him in, knowing he meant it with all his soul.

"I CAN'T BELIEVE SHE'S REALLY NOT LETTING US GO out to find dresses," Novalie whined as we walked between classes. Normally I'd be training with Cal at this time, but I wasn't ready to see him yet. So, I was just following Novalie to all of her classes instead. "We should have looked for some that time we went to talk to Cal."

"You could always go anyway," I said, like the typically bad influence that I was. "She can't keep track of everyone. Or just get something delivered."

She sighed. "I guess. I just want to look my best if I'm going to see my parents for the first time in what, fourteen years?"

"Want to skip next class?" I tried to change the subject, not particularly wanting to think about my own heritage right then, especially with my dream fresh in my mind.

"Sure," Novalie said easily. "What do you want to do instead?"

252

"I propose an experiment." She shot me a look of interest and I smirked. "How much alcohol does it take to get an undead vampire drunk?"

"A lot," Emerson said, matter of fact as she seemed to appear out of thin air. She shrugged when we looked at her in shock. "I read."

"Well, good thing I have more than enough to go around," Novalie said smugly and I gaped at her as we reached my room.

"When did you have time to pick up booze?"

She shrugged. "The debut might be important yada yada, but it's a party at the end of the day and I do *not* go to a party without having pre-drinks first."

"Wise," Emerson remarked and I snorted, pushing open my door and freezing when I saw what was laid out on the bed.

"Am I seeing things," I said slowly, walking inside, "or are there three gorgeous dresses on my bed?"

Novalie squealed, clapping her hands together as she hurried over to look at them. Emerson closed the door behind us and I joined Novalie at the bed.

The first dress had a high collar studded with black gems that glinted when I picked it up. There were no sleeves, and the front of the dress was a triangular shape that would emphasise my waist, made up of an intricate dark lace interwoven with more glittering black gems. The skirt flared out into some kind of sheer tulle and a note fell to the floor as I admired it.

Wear the black set.

I grinned. Hayes. I knew exactly what he was talking about—he seemed to like buying me lingerie and nightwear, more of it randomly showed up in my room intermittently.

The most recent had been a matching black lace set that had sheer cups and sheer knickers with optional garter clips that I'd probably go without.

"These look tailored," Novalie said, admiration clear in her voice as she held up a red dress that bordered on black.

"Boy's got connections," Emerson added, eyeing the last dress. "I don't want to know how he got our measurements though, do I."

We laughed and Novalie left to grab the drinks she'd squirrelled away in her room.

"Do you like it?" I said quietly as Emerson hesitantly touched the dress meant for her. It was a pale lilac with gold accents forming a shimmering corset effect and sheer loops to rest on the sides of her arms.

"It's beautiful," she admitted and I beamed. "I'm just not sure what point there is to me attending the debut. I obviously won't have any family there."

"You're wrong," I said steadily, looking down at my dress and thinking about what I might do with my hair. "I'll be there. We made history, you and I. A new sire line. They're going to want to look at us—and I say let them stare. Stuffy bastards won't know what hit them."

Emerson laughed and I was happy to see her smiling—it couldn't have been easy leaving behind everything she knew for this life she hadn't asked for. But I knew she could go and see her family any time once she was done at Ashvale, though eventually they'd notice that she wasn't ageing.

"Try and have fun tonight," I murmured as Novalie burst through my door, having used her foot to open it somehow because her arms were so full of bottles. "God. We're going to be on the floor before we even get to the debut."

∼

AS IT TURNED OUT, IT WAS SERIOUSLY FUCKING hard for an undead vampire to get so much as a buzz. Though, Novalie decided to take one for the team and get horrifically drunk so I could drink from her and experience a buzz that way. Even then, it wore off fast.

But I didn't need the alcohol, not really. For the first time since being at Ashvale and awakening as a vampire, I felt completely at home in my skin—like this was where I was meant to be all along. In this dress, with this man, and these friends.

"You look beautiful," Hayes leaned down to murmur as we queued to enter the hall.

"Thank you for the dresses, and for being here with me."

I wasn't sure I'd ever seen Hayes eyes as light as they were right then, before he leaned down to kiss me and I welcomed him eagerly. This was new for us, being so openly together. Everyone knew about the blood bond, but not everyone knew that we'd accepted it, and each other. We were much stronger together than we could ever be apart and, more than anything, it was nice to have someone who you knew would always be there. But in that moment, when we kissed, I felt less like a vampire and more like a princess. The credits would roll any second and this would be our happily ever after—but the reality was a little different. We were lining up for a ball filled with the most powerful undead vampires in our world. In this story, I was more likely to be the monster than the princess.

"Are you nervous?"

Hayes looked surprised. "No. Are you?"

"I already have all the family I need."

I wasn't sure how many vampires went unclaimed during the debut until their families decided they were 'worthy' enough, but I knew it was a lot. To me, that wasn't family. Family loved unconditionally, not just when you made it worth their while.

We made it to the front of the queue and there was a genuine announcer at the door that called my name. "Presenting, Leonora Romilly and her blood-chosen."

I looked to Hayes in surprise. "Why didn't they say your name?"

He shrugged. "I didn't give it to them. I prefer it that way. Less nosy vampires in my life."

I hadn't seen the ballroom since we'd been at Ashvale, it had been closed for renovations—presumably to prepare it for the ball. It was bigger than I could have imagined and already there was an undercurrent in the air that sent a ripple of awareness over my skin. A band stood on a raised podium, playing something surprisingly upbeat and living vampires mingled with the undead freely. Lark never could have described the energy in this room accurately. It felt.... Wild.

"So how does this claiming thing work anyway?" I muttered and Hayes looked around disinterestedly, giving me the chance to fully ogle him in his tux.

"If they like what they see here and what they've heard from their spies, you'll receive an invitation after the ball." He looked at me and smirked when he found my eyes still on him. "Do *you* see something you like?"

I rolled my eyes but couldn't stop the slight smile from coming out. I did like what I saw—Hayes was *made* for a tux, it emphasised all of his strong, cutting features and made them look regal.

Novalie was already mingling, charming vampires all

around her, and even Emerson was dancing with someone I didn't recognise.

"Dance with me," Hayes said suddenly and didn't wait for a reply before tugging me closer, his hands finding my waist to pull me into position and then drifting up my skin to capture one of my hands in his.

He twirled me effortlessly and I knew my mouth had to be hanging open. I never would have expected Hayes to be good at this kind of thing, and he was clearly enjoying the shock on my face. A chuckle reverberated through him and into me because of how close we stood, and when his lips brushed the shell of my ear I shivered.

Hayes danced like he fought—lethal precision and grace, every movement sinuous, driving me wild as his hands seemed to be everywhere, brushing the inside of my bare arm, scalding through the material of my dress on my waist, sliding up the back of my neck—

I slapped his hand away. "Do you know how long it took to get my hair to do this? Don't touch it." A teasing grin curled around his mouth and I slapped his chest lightly. "*No!* Don't even think about it."

He spun me in an elaborate twirl and dip that made me laugh as he led me around the room.

"I don't suppose you might allow me to cut in?" A smooth voice asked when we paused in front of the band.

I looked up into a face that unnerved me. It was young, early forties at most, but his eyes... they were ancient.

Hayes inclined his head slightly and the other man scrutinised him for a second before Hayes disappeared into the bodies surrounding us.

"Leonora Romilly," the man said. "I've been waiting to meet you. I've heard such interesting things."

I accepted his hand cautiously and allowed him to steer us into a dance. "I'm sorry, could I ask who I have the pleasure of dancing with?"

His smile faded slightly before burning bright once more. "Of course, my dear. I'd heard you had sustained heavy memory loss. I am Adrian Curio, head of the council."

Well, fuck. It was lucky he hadn't ended me right there for not knowing who he was.

I paused our dance to bow deeply. "A pleasure."

The sparkle was back in his eyes when I rose. Ego was always the way with these kinds of men. "The pleasure is all mine. I think we can expect very interesting things of you in the future." He stepped back and I bowed my head once more. "I can't be seen to be playing favourites, so I must now take my leave. But before I do, who was that young man you were dancing with when I arrived?"

I opened my mouth to reply, but then Hayes' words about nosy vampires in his life flashed through my head and I smiled tightly. "My blood-chosen."

Adrian raised an eyebrow but didn't press for more information than that.

"Enjoy the party, Leonora."

"You too," I murmured and immediately sought out Hayes after the head of the council departed and I watched as he swept his way over to Elowen.

I couldn't spot Hayes' blond head anywhere, but I did catch a glimpse of Rowan so I made my way over to him instead.

"You're late," I teased and he chuckled.

"Fashionably.

"If you say so." I held out my hand. "Want to dance?"

"Love to."

He wasn't as good as Hayes at dancing, but it was pleasant enough. We did a couple of turns about the room before I spotted Emerson off to the side looking uncomfortable so we made our way over to her.

"You okay?"

She nodded. "Yeah, I guess just being here really puts it all into perspective. This is my life now. I'm a vampire. And a vampire outcast at that."

"You're not an outcast," Rowan said sharply and I nodded. "You're just more special than them all and they hate it. Something rare. Vampires turned and not born used to be considered to be on the same level as royalty."

"What changed?" she whispered and I looked to Rowan, curious myself.

He shrugged. "Nothing, they just became more rare. Turned vampires can't procreate, like a living vampire does, and they also can't turn through their bite. Plus, the amount of vampires who can turn by bite is small. All of that just led to fewer turned vampires."

We both stared at him with wide eyes before I turned to Emerson challengingly. "Maybe it's time to remind them where they stand."

Her chin lifted and I felt a smug pride as she walked off with a confidence that made several nearby vampires stop and stare. The crowd parted for her and we watched her go in an admiring silence.

"What are we looking at?"

I jumped and turned around. "There you are! Where did you go?"

"I was hiding from Adrian."

"Not a fan?"

Hayes' smile was tight. "I would be a fan of holding his

still beating heart in the palm of my hand and crushing it between my fingers."

"Descriptive," I remarked and then took his hand in mine. "Come on, dance with me again." I paused and grabbed Rowan. "You too."

We moved closer to the band and I stood between them, dancing to a cover of a pop song I vaguely recognised but couldn't place. The room was warm and with them on either side of me I felt safe, loved, protected.

I raised my hands in the air, swaying to the drums as the lead singer crooned words I couldn't make out. It felt like my blood was humming, my body balanced on the knife's edge of overly sensitised gooseflesh.

I wasn't sure when we'd moved so close together, but Hayes' chest was against mine, his mouth and cheek brushing my own. Rowan was at my back, one hand wrapped around my waist and his mouth brushing the nape of my neck.

The beat turned heady and I sighed when lips brushed my neck and hands stroked down my arms. My eyes fluttered open and I watched, entranced, as an undead vampire in front of us slid to his knees, lifting his dance partner's skirt and pulling her underwear to one side, baring her to the room. I couldn't look away as his fingers parted her pussy lips, slicking through them twice until his mouth followed the path of his fingers.

The scent of blood reached me and I looked to my right just as Novalie plunged her fangs into Emerson's neck. Emerson swayed in her arms, her back arching against Novalie's front. I blinked and a different set of vampires took their place as I danced slowly between Hayes and Rowan.

Two male vampires had their hands fisted in each other's

shirts as they kissed passionately while two others sank to their knees in front of them and unzipped their trousers.

I could only assume this was the part of the night that Lark had tried to warn us about—when bloodlust tipped over from so many undead vampires in one room, the power lowering everyone's inhibitions as the blood flowed freely.

Lips brushed my neck and I sighed with pleasure, pulling my gaze away from the couple fucking against the wall while another vampire watched, his dick in his hand.

Hayes kissed the point where my pulse would have been and when he bit down, a slow sink of his teeth, I shuddered in Rowan's arms. I could feel him, hard against my arse and Hayes firm at my front. I tilted my head and Rowan hesitated before placing a kiss on the exposed arch of my throat, his tongue flicking across the skin there slowly. Hayes pulled from me and I panted, grinding myself between them until Rowan joined him, his teeth sending double hits of pleasure through me as they drank from me in tandem. Their heads lifted and I watched as they kissed over my shoulder, my blood staining their mouths before Rowan pulled away and bent back to my neck.

I lost myself in the sensation as Hayes stroked my breasts through my dress, my nipples quickly hardening. I opened my eyes, wanting to watch, and instead saw Rowan lift his face, his mouth dripping red and sending a bolt of fear through me as the slice of memory I'd dreamed suddenly roared to the front of my mind.

Hayes' head jerked up and looked at me in concern. The image faded and I breathed easy again but Rowan took a step back, licking his lips clean.

"I think I'm done for the night."

"You don't have to—"

"Goodnight." He walked away and a brief clarity came back to me as I watched him go, until the fog of lust clouded my brain and Hayes resumed the kisses he was pressing to my neck.

More vampires were in a state of undress than clothed now, the scent of blood heavy in the air. I didn't want to be watched, not in the way that some of the vampires were on display, but—

Hayes took my hand and pulled us closer to one of the shadowy alcoves at the edge of the hall. They were dimly lit by candlelight but the sounds of other vampires reached us as the slap of skin on skin and throaty moans echoed through the space.

My hands were greedy as they found his shoulders, touching and tugging and wanting *more*. I knew he was happy to oblige. Hayes reached down and freed his dick from his trousers, stroking it once, twice, and I could feel the ache moving through him. I dropped to my knees and took him in my mouth, swallowing him down in almost one go and salivating at the taste of him, sweet and salty in my mouth. I worked him to the edge and then stood, letting my mouth trail off of his hard length, my tongue flicking over his tip in one last tease.

The wet sound of fucking emerged somewhere on our right and two unmistakably male grunts followed the high moans of a woman clearly having the time of her life.

"You want to put on a show?" Hayes said, his voice dark and wicked in my ear. "You want them to hear but not see?"

I nodded and he smiled, his hand reaching behind me to unzip my dress, his gaze darkening when he saw the set I'd worn at his instruction.

"I need to taste you," he growled and I parted my legs as

he knelt between them, his tongue sliding over me wetly and making my clit throb. I yelped as he guided me down onto his face as he laid back and at first I held myself back, not wanting to crush him, but his hands reached up and pulled me down onto his tongue with force and I moaned.

He tongue-fucked me and I knew the others could hear, the thought making it hotter even knowing they couldn't see anything. I came with a whimper, riding Hayes' face until he lifted me off of him and I felt him nudging against me.

A variety of moans filtered to us as Hayes lined himself up beneath me, pushing through my wetness until I was whimpering. I leaned down and bit him, drinking deeply and licking the excess from my mouth when I sat up.

His fingers found my clit and I gasped, rolling my hips to meet him and then crying out when his dick filled my arse and not my pussy.

"It's a shame Rowan left early." Hayes groaned as he thrust into me harder, faster, his fingers finding my pussy and slipping inside. "We could have filled you so good."

The sex was frenzied, a true fucking, his hips slamming up to mine as his fingers pulsed against my inner wall. Before I could process it, I'd clamped down around him and was coming so hard I was sure I'd blacked out for a second.

"Did you enjoy that, love?" Hayes asked a second later after he'd finished inside me.

"Yes," I said, exhausted like I'd just run a marathon.

"Let's get you to bed," he said quietly, and I didn't protest when he picked me up and carried me out of the shadows and back into the light.

Chapter Twenty-Eight

I woke up cradled to Hayes' chest, his warmth relaxing me even as his proximity awoke other feelings.

"Morning," he murmured and I smiled, pressing a kiss to his chest as I rolled away.

"No," he groaned. "Where are you going?"

"Shower," I said, a teasing smile on my mouth, "somebody had me on my knees in a filthy alcove."

He looked smug at the reminder and I laughed, detouring to the door when someone knocked—or hammered on it was more accurate.

"Thank fuck you're okay," Novalie said as she brushed past me with Emerson and Rowan on her tail.

"Why wouldn't I be okay?" I gave Hayes a confused look and snorted when I saw he'd pulled his covers and pillow over his head.

"They found an undead vampire this morning," Emerson said quietly, "drained of all their blood."

Hayes peeked out of the covers, a flicker of hope in his eyes. "Was it Adrian Curio?"

"Nobody knows who it is," Novalie said, throwing her hands into the air. "That's why we all ran over here to check on the undead vampire we all actually give a shit about."

I bit my lip on a smile. "Thank you."

"Another murder though," Emerson said, shaking her head, sparkly makeup still smudged around her eyelids.

We all fell silent and Hayes sighed. "Well, I guess I'm awake now. I'll call Cal. An undead vampire changes things."

"How so?" Rowan said, a sharpness to his voice that made me narrow my eyes.

"Well, firstly, it means Elowen didn't do shit with the information we gave her. Nobody left the grounds, supposedly, so whoever is responsible is still in the castle."

"Plus, an undead vampire?" Novalie shuddered. "They would have to be strong to overpower one of them, or be taking the drug, which means they're connected."

"Or very hungry," I murmured and Emerson nodded a haunted look on her face that made me want to rip whoever was doing this limb from limb.

"It's also an escalation," Hayes said, putting his phone down after sending a text off. "This person either doesn't care about the consequences, or just needs more—more blood, more power, we won't know yet."

"When do you think we will know?" Rowan asked and Hayes shrugged.

"When they kill again."

"We should have some time before that happens though, right? If they only just fed and fed well?"

Cal appeared and had clearly heard my questions. "Or

they'll feed more quickly if their hunger is getting worse—bad enough that they took on an undead vampire."

I looked away from him but nodded. "Wait, you said he was dead? Surely just draining an undead of their blood wouldn't kill them?"

Novalie swallowed. "The missing blood just pointed to a vampire. But they found him in pieces. Ripped apart, heart chomped on like the one on the top floor a few weeks ago."

Fuck. Whatever was happening to this person, they weren't messing around.

"So you think they'll kill again tonight?" Hayes asked the mage—I refused to call him *dad*. Hayes sent me a look that told me to play nice and I rolled my eyes.

"I'd stake my life on it," Cal said and I hummed.

"A mage has to have more magick than an undead vampire right? Making your blood even richer? So maybe we should use you as bait."

"Or you," Cal shot back and I grimaced.

"What's that supposed to mean?" Novalie demanded and I glared at the mage for letting the cat out of the bag. He just smirked and god if I hadn't seen that expression on my own damn face.

"Meet Daddy dearest," I said dryly and Emerson's mouth fell open.

"You're joking," Rowan said and I shook my head, keeping my words inside in an effort to be nice for Hayes' sake.

"Anyway, we're all under house arrest," Novalie continued, looking back between me and Cal as if cataloguing our similarities like our curls, our mouth, and god knows what else.

"Anyone found wandering will automatically be under suspicion."

I swore. "Well what are you all doing here then? Get back to your rooms before Elowen decides to kill one of you off for being out where you're not supposed to be."

Emerson winced. "We wanted to—"

"Check on me, I know. " I shook my head. "Hayes has a phone. Call or text next time. Besides, if I was dead, it would be too late for me but you could save yourselves."

They filed out, looking a little chastised, until it was just the three of us left.

"Well this is awkward," I muttered and Hayes stood up and walked into the bathroom, closing the door behind him.

Traitor, I thought and felt his amusement.

"Did you ever look for me?" I asked bluntly and Cal blinked, clearly taken aback by the abrupt questioning.

"I told you, I thought—"

"I was dead, yeah. I heard you before—but after my mother took off, did you not ever wonder?"

"Maybe it makes me naive, but I didn't think she'd lie about something like that. I thought she left because, like me, she was grieving the loss of our unborn child."

I fell silent, watching the emotions play out over his face as he sat down heavily on the bed. "If I could go back and look for you, I would. I wouldn't have let them send you away, out into the world to be killed. You would have had a family, and I would have killed before I let this be your life—but I didn't get the choice and neither did you." He scrubbed a hand down his face and when he looked at me I could see the truth in his eyes. "If you need to hate me, I understand. But just know that I'll take whatever you can give me. I wasn't there before, but I can be now—if you'll let me."

I knew Hayes was listening, knew what he thought I should say or do—but this was my life and it had to be my decision. "I don't know how I feel. I don't know if I ever missed you, or wondered about you, because I don't remember my life. I think I need time, but I'll try to be less of a dick to you. Just don't start holding back with me in training just because I'm your kid."

His lips tipped up at the corners and I half-smiled back.

"There, was that so hard?" Hayes said as he strolled out of the bathroom.

"Prick," I said, throwing an orb of water at him that he deflected easily and Cal frowned.

"I didn't teach you that one."

I shrugged. "Figured it was the same principle as the light."

"Well, just be careful. I don't want you biting off more than you can chew."

"Noted."

Hayes was typing on his phone again and when he looked up, his face was grim. "They've named the vamp—Montlake."

"Is that bad?" I wondered aloud and Hayes nodded.

"He's the second most powerful vampire on the council. Or, well, I suppose he was..."

"They're probably in uproar," Cal said quietly and I tended to agree. "Stay here. Don't draw attention to yourselves. Be safe."

"Where are you going?"

Cal looked at me and there was something in his eyes I'd never seen before. Pride? Affection? I couldn't tell. "I'll be back, don't worry. Just stay alive until then. Okay?"

We both nodded and Cal smiled before vanishing.

"Fuck, I really need him to teach me how to do that soon."

"Let's just focus on keeping you from becoming a snack," Hayes said dryly and I raised an eyebrow. "Well, he may have been a dick about it but Cal had a point—you *are* half-mage. So that probably makes you the tastiest thing in the castle."

Great.

CHAPTER TWENTY-NINE

Teeth glinted red and a smile stretched too wide as full lips pulled back over teeth that weren't right. Too long, too sharp. I'd screamed—I remembered that now. There had been a dazed moment of confusion when I'd hit the ground, my head thumping down on the pavement and stunning me. It was all the time the monster needed to bury its teeth in my throat, to slash and bite and growl until my head felt loose and the world darkened around me.

If I could still sweat, I was certain my body would have been covered in it as I woke up. Another partial memory. The same night. I just couldn't see their damned *face*. As it was, I was shaking and I felt around in the covers for Hayes, nausea hitting me when his familiar form didn't appear.

I had no reason to think anything was wrong, he might have just gone for a night-time walk, but why would he take the risk when Elowen and the council were on the warpath?

No. Something didn't feel right. I swung my legs out of bed and crept over to the window, peering outside. Nothing looked amiss, there was no struggle in our room and I was certain one would have woken me up anyway. All I could see outside was moonlight, trees and mist.

I focused on the beat in my chest that was Hayes and could sense him out in the forest, which seemed odd for this time of night. Maybe he'd discovered something? Or had received a message? His phone was on the bedside table, so I picked it up and scrolled through, nothing particularly standing out. My thumb hovered over Cal's name before deciding against calling him. I didn't know for sure that anything was wrong.

Still, I pulled on a pair of joggers and one of Hayes' grey tees as well as my boots and slipped quietly out of the door.

The castle was dead silent in a way that unnerved me. I could hear no signs of life as I moved around and I wondered if many people had air shields surrounding their doors like the one Hayes could conjure. But why?

I made my way down the stairs quickly and quietly, and paused when a figure emerged up ahead.

Adrian.

I hung back as he patrolled the corridor. Now it made more sense why everyone was so silent—nobody wanted to draw the unwanted attention of the council. Not when they were on a literal vampire hunt.

Once Adrian was out of sight, I crept onwards, heading out across the grass and into the trees that stood dark against the sky.

The pulse that drew me to Hayes told me he was in the centre somewhere and I felt it guide me as I moved, the wind brisk against my unaffected skin and the smell of damp earth worrying instead of soothing me—it smelled like a graveyard.

A strange sound reached me and I paused, curious.

According to the bond, it wasn't Hayes. Somebody else was out here tonight too.

I followed the sound and emerged at the edge of the woods where the clearing break stood. The clouds parted and I could see a little better, my body freezing up as I tried to take it all in.

The sound I'd heard was sobs. The figure up ahead was shaking as they cried and the rhythmic sounds of dirt hitting flesh made my stomach turn as I took one step forward.

I'd made no noise, but whatever they were hopped up on clearly boosted their hearing and gods knew what else. This person might have taken on an undead vampire and lived. Had obliterated them.

I took another step forward and their body stiffened, halting their digging.

There was something familiar about the silhouette—which made sense, I'd probably walked by them at Ashvale. Their head was bowed and as they raised it, a small cry escaped my mouth.

"I'm sorry, Leonora. I never wanted this. She made me take it—I wanted to be strong. I didn't know it would make me into this. Make me *hurt* people."

"Rowan," I choked out, clutching my hands to the bottom of my throat as I tried to understand what I was seeing. "What are you doing? What's happened?"

"I killed them," he said, sniffing and looking out into the distance with a boyish wonder that I used as a distraction to move closer. "Once you start taking it, you can't stop. I tried, I tried, but it just doesn't work. It makes you do it."

His hands ran through his hair, leaving it sticking up at odd angles and flecked with dirt. Blood smeared his mouth and the sight of it made me shudder, my dream fresh in my mind.

I took another step closer. "Why don't you come back to the castle with me? We can figure this out."

"*Don't*," he roared and I froze. "Don't come any closer. I don't want to do this again. I don't want to hurt anyone else."

I raised my hands in supplication. "Okay, okay. What if I go back and bring help?"

"No. No. You can't leave. You'll tell. You won't have a choice. Can't let you leave, can't let you stay," he said, his words coming quicker and quicker until they were slurred together. "I'm sorry," he breathed. "I think I have to kill you again."

Again. No.

"What did you say?"

It was like Rowan wasn't even present, the drugs completely overriding his system. "I hated it. You were so nice... I liked your orange jumper but then you fell and it was red."

Red. Bleeding into the sky. I tried to breathe and couldn't, my limbs shaking. "Rowan—"

"It was just chance. The pub was small and you were... beautiful. I didn't know who you were—*what* you were," he babbled and I wasn't sure I could hear any more of this. "And then there you were. Whole."

You're a vampire. That's what he'd said to me the moment he'd seen me for the first time. I'd thought it was weird but harmless, but now I understood. He'd come back to Ashvale, to Hayes, and his victim had followed him there. Haunting him. He'd known who I was and what had happened to me all along.

"Did you make the drugs?" I said, trying to keep a leash on my temper, trying to breathe.

"No, no, no," he said, becoming incoherent again as he looked out at the trees, jumping when he looked back and saw me again. "This is your fault."

"What?" I swallowed my shock and tried to bottle my anger, feeling Hayes' presence growing nearer, but it was hard. Every time I looked at him I saw him in the library, smiling at me, or the way he'd seemed concerned when I'd spoken about needing to know who I was, what had done this to me. He had *lied*. Over and over.

My fangs ached and I shook my head, gritting my teeth. "Who gave you the drugs?"

Rowan looked baffled, his eyebrows drawing together as he squinted at me. "You did, Elowen."

Shock and satisfaction were a strange mix inside me. I knew I'd been onto something with her but this?

"You did this to me," Rowan continued, his voice turning into a low snarl as the hunger gripped him again and I swore as I realised he'd slipped into a drug-fueled delusion. Was this how he'd looked on the night I'd died? "Why did you make me a monster?"

"I didn't," I said, trying desperately to hold on to my self-control for the sake of the friendship we'd had and he roared, charging at me.

"Liar!"

A flash of silver darted past me, intercepting Rowan and throwing him to the ground.

The silver wolf.

I wasn't sure why it had decided to protect me now, when it had seemed like it might want to eat me before, but I couldn't look a gift horse in the mouth. I had to find Hayes and go. I looked around frantically, seeing only more trees and shadow. But the bond seemed sure he was already here, I'd become good at reading it the past few weeks so I couldn't understand why—

The wolf snarled and then whined when Rowan landed a savage punch before shooting me a look, and I froze when I met the familiar pair of icy blue eyes. Hayes. Hayes was the *fucking wolf.*

Run, he managed to tell me, the words strangely distorted like it was hard for him to think in human patterns while in that form, but I didn't stay to ask questions—I just did as he'd told me: I ran.

CHAPTER THIRTY

THE TREES WHIPPED AT MY ARMS AS I RAN BUT I felt numb. Rowan. All along. It still didn't make sense in my mind. How could he have been hiding this the whole time? Then again, there had been several times where he'd done or said something questionable—and Hayes himself had said Rowan had seemed different recently.

Wetness hit my cheeks and I touched them in shock. How could this be happening? How could the guy who'd kissed me in relief when he'd found me alive after that magickal overdose have tried to kill me? Even if it was the result of drugs? The guy who read in the library and studied literature? Who thought reading philosophy books was fun?

Before I knew what was happening, I'd stopped running and was instead bent over sobbing in the dark.

Elowen. He'd said Elowen had done this—had made him into a monster. I knew I should wait. Knew Hayes would be pissed beyond belief that I'd charged off ahead, but Rowan hadn't been the only one keeping secrets.

I shook my head as I started running again, my mind

replaying the moment that wolf—*Hayes*—had burst into the clearing.

A silver wolf, I realised. Surely not. The missing child from the royal line—it couldn't be Hayes, could it?

Rage flooded me and I let it fuel me as I ran faster than I ever had before. Did I actually know anybody I'd thought was my friend? My family?

The mage was my dad, my... Hayes, was a wolf, and maybe a prince? And Rowan.. he was a murderer and a liar.

I burst into Elowen's office without stopping or slowing, the door flying off its hinges and she looked up at me in surprise.

"Leonora—"

"Shut up," I told her, putting as much power as I could behind the command and growling when it only held for a moment before Elowen shook it off, her anger a white fire spreading across her face.

Her desk was scattered with papers and the rug beneath my feet was spotless except for my muddy footprints

"I knew you were lying," I began as rage made me tremble. "But I couldn't have guessed it was this."

"I don't know what you mean—"

"The drugs. Rowan. The murders. Why? Why supply it?"

All pretences dropped, her face smoothed out. "I don't have to explain myself to you."

"The fuck you dont! You're the reason I'm dead!"

She stared at me for a second and then began talking. "Well, actually I think you'll find that Rowan is the reason you're dead."

I squeezed my eyes closed as my vision filled with red, rage raising its ugly head.

"The drug increases the abilities of the living vampires to that of an undead, as I'm sure you've worked out by now, but it also increases their thirst, an unfortunate side effect."

Unfortunate—that was how she described the deaths of all those students, and god knows how many we didn't know about. That's how she described *my* death. *Emerson's!*

"The first batch proved to be too strong, unbalanced. Highly addictive. I had to keep supplying the initial test subjects, otherwise they completely went off the rails and would be of no use to me."

"You were—what? Trying to create a loyal little army?"

"Something like that."

I grit my teeth, trying to hold on to my humanity even as I teetered on the edge. "And Rowan? Which batch was he on?"

Her eyes glinted and I knew what she was going to say before she opened her mouth. "The first."

"Why keep them alive in the first place? Why not just kill them and be done with it if they were such a liability?" My voice was harsh and I tried to use my anger to numb my other emotions out as I questioned her on why she hadn't been more callous. Why she'd spared Rowan and the others.

She raised and dropped one delicate shoulder. "It was prudent to know some of the other long term side effects."

"You're a fucking monster," I growled and she smiled like it was a compliment.

"We can't help our natures," she said and I tilted my head.

"Lie."

"What?"

"You're lying—you weren't always like this, were you? "

Her jaw clenched and she shook her head. "You know, your father used to do the exact same thing."

All thoughts left my head as I stared at her in shock. "What did you say?" I whispered and her smile was cruel, like she knew I couldn't handle anything else right then.

"I'll admit, your level of power pleases me. If you hadn't failed the most basic of tests, maybe I would have claimed you. But you couldn't do that one key thing: *survive*."

"I'm here, aren't I?"

"Because of *me*." I blinked and she laughed, it sounded rusty, like it had been so long she couldn't remember how to do it. "You asked me before and looked so doubtful I thought you were going to call me on it right then and there." She shook her head with a snort. "*Lie*," she mimicked. "But you didn't. The only reason you made it here is because I made sure you were found. Made sure you had fresh blood close by."

"You called in the retrieval," I murmured before looking up, a snarl on my lips. "The lake?" I wasn't sure if I could feel the floor under my feet as something beyond anger raised its head. "You put that girl there?"

Elowen looked at me, a small smile playing on her lips. "Drown," she instructed me, the thrall in her voice strong but I batted it aside. She had killed her, had put her in my way knowing I would lose control.

"If you cared so little, why take the time to save me?"

Elowen rounded the desk, each step precise and I kept my eyes on her.

"It seemed only fair. I was the reason you were killed after all."

Tit for tat. That was the extent of her motherly love.

"Why?" I said hoarsely and cleared my throat. "Why leave Cal? Why hide me?"

If she was surprised I knew about Cal, she didn't show it. All this time, she'd been right here under his nose. "Because the change made me different—he loved the old me. Not who I'd become. I knew he'd want to give you the chance to choose—vampire tradition or life as a mage. I didn't want you to waste that potential. Of course, I ended up disappointed anyway."

Bitch. "I'm going to kill you," I said simply, the anger and despair and sheer wrath inside of me filling every crevice of my being until I almost felt numb and she laughed again.

"You finally work out who your sire line is and you decide to kill me? Your own mother?"

I flinched. "You are not my mother. Not after everything you've done. Not after what you did to Rowan. What you made him do to me."

She tilted her head like a cat eyeing up its prey. "Interesting that you still hold such commitment to him. I told him what the possible side effects were, I told him to stay at Ashvale. He decided power was more important than potential casualties. But here you are, so loyal."

I snarled. "And who else should I be loyal to? You?" I laughed. "I suppose you're where I get my lack of sentimentality from." I could feel the storm inside of me, lightning bubbling through my breaths til I could taste smoke on my tongue. If what she was saying was true—and I could see no reason why she'd start lying now—then Rowan had known exactly what he was doing with that drug. He'd known, and he'd done it anyway. Just like he'd pretended to be my friend whilst hiding the fact that he was my murderer.

"You are probably the biggest disappointment of my

life," Elowen spat and I laughed again, feeling sparks jump up my throat and flash in the air as I slowly lost control.

I felt nothing. Cared about nothing. I was pain and anger and thunder personified.

"You know, I bet Adrian thinks the same thing about you. He is your sire right?" Her eyes widened and I chuckled at that shot in the dark paying off. "I thought so, considering the interest he took in me at the debut. I think I saw him in the corridors earlier, maybe we should let him in on this little conversation." I gestured to the doorway and laughed when Elowen's hand closed around my throat.

"And to think," she whispered, her voice like venom, "you could have been something. Had everything."

Her hand tightened and I shook with silent laughter—it wasn't like I had to breathe after all.

"A waste," she proclaimed, dropping me and following up her sentiment with a stinging slap that made my ears ring.

"I agree," I said with a sneer, snapping my hand out towards her face as I cast an orb of water with my other, flinging it at her head and adding heat at the last moment. The smell of burning flesh made my nose wrinkle but Elowen barely flinched.

"Well, now you've just pissed me off." Her fist crashed into my face, my ribs, but once she moved close enough I snapped my head up and into hers, delighting in the crunch of bone as she swore.

"You little bitch."

"I am my mother's daughter." Elowen snarled and I beckoned her forwards. "You know, I think you would look so much better with some colour in your cheeks."

Her eyes narrowed and I smiled as I clasped my hands forward and thought of heat, of the anger churning like an inferno in my chest. Lightning burst into being and flowed through the wave of light I cast. Elowen screamed, her hair catching alight and I watched, fascinated as the flames spread easily across her shoulders until she managed to summon her own magic—a combination of water and air to smother the flames. Maybe I should have taken Cal's advice and ran while she was distracted, but it was too late. She leapt for me, unhinged and feral, her lips peeled back from her teeth and hands curved into claws reaching for my chest.

A snarl from the entrance made us both look up. The low rumble sent shivers down my spine as the hulking figure of the wolf filled the doorway.

"Impossible," Elowen gasped and then the wolf leapt for her, missing her throat by mere inches as she ran, revenge forgotten in her desire to flee.

Her shoulder struck me and I flew backwards, my head knocking into the wall until I saw stars. No, not stars, teeth —stretching wide in a smile turned snarl, brown eyes turning cold, hungry as Rowan leapt for my throat, pinning me to the floor and sobbing as he drank, apologising as he bit near-clean through my neck, white teeth floating in the dark until my eyes flew open and blue eyes, not brown, stared down at me.

Elowen was gone and I stared at Hayes, half-wishing I'd never remembered, half-wishing I'd never wanted to. Because I knew who I was, knew what I would do. Even if it broke Hayes' heart. Even if it broke mine. Maybe if I hadn't remembered... Maybe if he hadn't lied...

"Rowan," I said and Hayes shook his head.

"No. No, it's not possible. Leonora, no. You're wrong."

"Rowan," I said again as the rest of the rage I'd known was waiting came flooding in. Everything that had happened, everything I'd lost... and he'd had the guts to become my friend, even knowing what he'd done. To kiss me. To *bite* me, like the last time he'd done so he hadn't stolen my life.

I stood and Hayes gripped my arm. "Whatever you think you have to do, you don't." He was completely naked from his shift back into his human form and I smiled without humour.

"I don't think you can really lecture me right now. Not when you're just as much of a liar as he is."

"Leonora—"

"He fucking killed me, Hayes! He murdered me and then befriended me like it wasn't fucked up. He lied even though he knew how much it was hurting me not to know what had happened or who I was. He was *never* my friend."

"I know," he said quietly. "But I can't let you do this, whatever you're planning. Not for his sake, but for yours."

I ignored his words and moved towards the door, snarling when he caught my arm. "This is the only warning I'll give you. *Let go.*"

He didn't move, just tried to dissuade me one more time and I exhaled sharply.

"I'm sorry."

His eyes widened but it was too late. My hand flashed out, connecting with his temple, and Hayes sank to the floor, unconscious as I walked away.

CHAPTER THIRTY-ONE

HAYES

I WOKE ALONE, NAKED, AND CONFUSED BY MY presence in Elowen's smashed up office. But then I remembered. Rowan. Leonora. The look in her green eyes as she'd taken me down.

I scrambled upright and winced at the throbbing pain in my head. I could feel her even now, just about. A warmth near my heart that had drawn me in as soon as I'd seen her—before I'd even understood what it was, before she'd ever tasted my blood. We had been inevitable and I worried that she might make a mistake she couldn't undo.

I swore as I tried to shift and nearly vomited. I was low on energy and blood and my magick wasn't as unlimited as Leonora's seemed to be. I settled for jogging as quickly as I could towards Rowan's room.

I could only hope I got there in time to stop her, or join her. I was furious at Rowan too—but I knew him. He was good to his core and I didn't want Leonora to do something she might regret. The very least I could do for her was let it be my soul that carried the weight of Rowan's retribution.

By the time we'd left the woods, he'd been back in his right mind, the hold the drug had on him fading. There was still hope for him—even if he'd done something unforgivable. I stopped on the third floor, turning to Rowan's room and swearing when I heard raised voices.

Adrian came around the corner of the corridor and his eyes flew wide when he saw me, taking my arm in his. I attempted to push past him but couldn't budge the grip he had on my arm in my weakened state.

"What the hell are you—?"

I didn't have time for this. I snarled, letting my eyes flash silver for the first time since I'd awoken and come to Ashvale. He jumped, dropping my arm immediately.

"You—"

I ran towards the open doorway, knowing Adrian was following behind me, and breathed a sigh of relief when I saw Leonora standing in front of Rowan. Alive. They were both still alive.

"Leonora," I gasped, breathless from relief and my stomach dropping when she didn't turn, like she couldn't hear me.

Tears dripped down Rowan's face as he found my eyes over her shoulder, a strange smell rising up in the air, just like—

Leonora's hand fell to her side and I stared at it in confusion.

It was coated in red.

Something was clasped between her fingers and she dropped it carelessly to the floor.

Heart, my brain told me, even as I struggled to process what I was seeing. *Rowan's heart.*

Leonora turned and met my eyes, feeling everything as it passed through me. My shock, my sorrow, my love.

Rowan fell to the floor, a hole in his chest where his heart should have been, and I watched it happen in slow motion.

Leonora stopped next to me in the doorway and barely spared Adrian a glance as she pushed past, her eyes briefly meeting mine before she turned away like she didn't recognise me.

"Sorry for the mess."

CONTINUE THE STORY IN LATE
2023/EARLY 2024 WITH...

ASHVALE

THE VAMPIRE'S KISS

Acknowledgments

I love vampires so bloody much, and if you're here then you probably do too! Thank you so much for reading and I'm sorry about that cliff-hanger... kind of. Book two will be out either at the end of the year or early in 2024 depending on some other publishing things that I can't talk about yet. I promise there is a HEA in sight though!

I'm sending so much love to Helena V Paris who has listened to me gush about this book incessantly, and for reading an earlier draft. Thanks also to Hannah Kaye and Noah Sky, my editors, your feedback helped make this book what it is today! Big thanks to Jess Amy and Mary Begletsova for the incredible artwork of Leonora and Hayes too.

Thank you to my ARC team and the bookish community for your interest in this book and your support in general, I'm forever grateful to you all <3

Finally, thank you to my agent, Erica Christensen, and Tantor media who will be producing the audio books for this series.

Want a sneak peek at my upcoming Friday 13th standalone release, One Last Touch? Read on!

About the Author

Jade Church is an avid reader and writer of spicy romance. She loves sweet and swoony love interests who aren't scared to smack your ass and bold female leads. Jade currently lives in the U.K. and spends the majority of her time reading and writing books, as well as binge re-watching *The Vampire Diaries*.

Friday, October 13th 2023...

ONE
LAST
TOUCH

Can love truly last beyond the grave?

CHAPTER ONE

I had never seen a ghost before I'd come to Alswell Manor. They were not ghosts in the way that I had been taught to see them, the way that we all had, as sheets with cut-outs and arms that were tented. No, these ghosts were the much more ordinary kind. A cup of tea left out on the side, not knowing it would never again be sipped. Dust motes that slipped through the air, waiting for a new breeze, a new breath. A painting, half-finished, the brushstrokes frozen, the paint congealing.

I, myself ,was haunted. I had made my way steadily through life like a ghost and I had to imagine that nothing much changed when you were dead. People would still speak over you, speed past you impatiently or cut you up while you walked as if you were never there, lost like a fingerprint, smudged on the lip of the Earth. But I hadn't known true loneliness until my mother, the only family I had left, faded out of existence. It was so strange to think that as you walked or talked or fucked or shopped, someone's last breath might be blowing right by you, and you would never know it.

It took a month for them to find her body. It wasn't unusual for us to go so long without talking, I had been away studying and I had assumed she was still off, travelling the world. But when I'd got the call, seen the unfamiliar number pop up on my phone, my blood had chilled. Somehow, I'd just known.

Though, of course, there were many things about my mother I didn't know. As it turned out, a lot more than I had ever expected. She had been found in a private cemetery, discovered by errant tourists travelling through the countryside on the way to the city and I hated that thought. That some strangers had been the one to find her, to see her in those last and infinitely private moments. But then again, better them than me. I preferred to remember her exactly as she'd been in life—slight, dark-haired, blue-eyed, graceful.

What was more shocking than the first call, was the second. My mother had no family except for me, but it seemed that wasn't always the case. Natalia Cole was actually Natalia Alswell and her inheritance became mine. My studies complete, about ten pounds to my name, what else could I do but pack up my meagre belongings into one, faded, suitcase and leave my student accommodation for the house that was now mine?

Warwickshire was quite the drive, though thankfully I wasn't the one who had to do it. I booked a cab, loaded my one suitcase into the boot and nodded at the driver before we lapsed into silence for the next two hours. Perfect.

It was raining and the quiet shush of the water over the windows lulled me almost to sleep, so I rolled it down to let the cool air in, soothing my skin and filling my nose with the familiar scent of wet earth and leaves. I didn't know what I was supposed to do when I got to the house. Had no clue if there would be someone there to greet me or show me around. I was pretty sure those kind of old houses had staff normally, but nobody had said anything to me about if that was the case at Alswell or if I might be expected to retain them. Though, thanks to my new inheritance, that wouldn't be a problem. It was kind of baffling really, but made a lot of sense when I thought about it—we'd always had money when I was growing up. Not ostentatious amounts or anything, but we were comfortable, we travelled, and when I decided to study my mum had paid for it rather than letting me take on student loans. I guess as a kid it hadn't been something I'd ever thought about. Lucky me.

The roads were relatively clear and the sky was a grey that bordered on blue, like it was still deciding whether or not to piss it down again and I rubbed my temples as they throbbed. I'd already signed over the deed for the house and got a key from the estate executor, I was just hoping the place was actually liveable. In hindsight, I probably should have looked it up before I'd decided to move in, but my tenancy was expiring and I'd been desperate. As long as it had a roof and four walls, how bad could it be?

The driver turned on the radio and hummed along absently to some pop song I'd probably have known if I'd bothered to go out to any of the pubs or clubs back in Reading. My interests had been elsewhere though, other than the occasional pint on a quiet afternoon, silently contemplating the people that passed around me and offering a smile to the pretty waitress that had worked there on Wednesday afternoons. It was an odd feeling, belonging and yet not, like running your gaze over a group of people and having the prickling sensation that something, some*one* was not quite right.

The trees outside the window were dense along the side of the road and the leaves bled into a stream of oranges and browns and greens that, while entirely unfamiliar, felt soothing somehow. Like something in my soul recognised these woods and this road. The driver had avoided the motorway as much as possible, which I couldn't fault him for really, as long as we got there I didn't mind which route he took.

I faced the front again, tugging errantly on the simple black gem stud in my ear as I caught a flash of my mismatched eyes in the rearview mirror. The driver looked up and jumped when he saw me staring back at him and I smiled wryly. I supposed it was fairly disconcerting if you weren't used to it—one of my eyes was the same shade as my mother's, a deep blue like the sea during a storm. The other was a perfect, almost clear, grey. My mum had said I was her little storm cloud, what with my dark hair, pale skin, and stormy eyes. I liked to think I looked a lot like her, something in the slant of my mouth, the tilt of my chin... But I suspected I looked a lot more like my father than she had been willing to admit . I'd never met him, had learned not to ask after I'd spent so long as a kid poking and squeezing, desperate to extract any little detail I could out of my mum. Of course, as a child, I hadn't noticed the sadness on her face, or the way she could hardly look at me for a day or two after I'd forced her into remembrance. It was that, more than anything else, that made me wonder if I looked like my father. If his eyes were grey too and I'd been formed as perfect halves of them both. Maybe Alswell Manor was my chance to find out the answers to those questions, the ones

I'd been too scared to ask my mum. And now she was dead and I would never get to ask her anything again.

My breath seemed to tighten in my chest and I bit into my cheeks so hard I tasted blood as I waited for the blur in my eyes to clear. I was *not* going to be one of those girls who cried in the back of a cab. I took a swig from the water bottle I'd brought with me and took a few more calming breaths before I noticed the car had been slowing and nervousness took me.

What if it was a shit tip? All overgrown and with a caved-in roof? Worse, what if there were squatters? Or bugs? Rats? Did they get rats in Warwickshire? The woods gave way and the cab drove along next to a tall, grey brick wall. It was obviously old, with green moss growing from between the cracks in the stone and the mortar. The car slowed even more as the wall curved around and a gate sat a little further back than the road, a mixture of dirt and gravel marking it as the entrance. There was another set of tyre tracks and footprints in the road dust and for a moment I couldn't pull my eyes away. Was this how she had gotten into the manor too? Were those the last footsteps my mother had made? More likely they were from the police and ambulance units, but still, it never hurt to dream, to imagine some last remnant of my mother imprinted and encased perfectly in the damp earth.

The cabbie pulled into the space and turned the car so its nose pointed outwards, ready to depart as soon as I climbed out. I tapped my card to his machine and tried not to wince at the cost, even if it was no longer a problem, old habits died hard. The air was colder than I'd expected it would be, as if the temperature had dropped ten degrees just by going a couple hours up the road, but I breathed it in, letting it sink into my lungs and cool my chest. In some ways, it felt like I had been cold ever since I'd got the news, like it had sunk its claws into me and refused to let go no matter how hard I burned or cried or screamed. She wasn't coming back, and only time would thaw the numbness that had seeped into me.

My case thudded down onto the gravel and I raised my hand in a final goodbye to the cabbie who nodded as his tyres skidded back out onto the main road.

It felt like the breeze here was familiar. Like the trees themselves groaned my name in a whispered hush that intermingled with the sound of rushing leaves. *Georgina. Georgina. Georgina.* I raised my eyes slowly, examining the gate thoroughly from the bottom to its top, stepping forward and brushing a finger over the places where the metal had begun to peel and rust. It was not ornate, which surprised me, it felt... solid. Like it was just there, as if it had sprouted out of the ground fully formed and ready to shelter its occupants. I left my case next to the seam and walked over to the footprints I'd seen from the car, squatting down and letting my hand rest against the dark dirt pressed flat by a petite shoe. Whether they were hers or not, I was still retracing the last steps my mother had ever made.

I pulled out the heavy key I'd been given by the estate executor. Apparently the manor didn't actually have its own key, there was only this one for the gate, so I would likely have to have my own cut. It squealed open and it felt like the wind hushed, like it was holding its breath alongside me as I stepped through and finally dared to look beyond at the house waiting for me. Alswell Manor. The place my mother had died. The place I could only assume I had been conceived.

The gate clanged shut behind me and the vibrations

rattled my teeth and all at once all sound rushed back. It was a wild unleashing of wind and leaves and birds and grass and somewhere in the distance I could hear the faint plink of water as the clouds opened up and rain began to drip down my face.

Georgina. It seemed to say. *Georgina, welcome home.*